Zero

For the small town of Lakewood, it began at Ed's Diner. A few customers were there, eating and talking. Ed was behind the counter, wiping at a stain that had been there longer than the waitresses. In roughly ten minutes, Ed would die screaming.

Ed idly wondered where Old Timmins, his fishing buddy, had gotten off to. *Probably on one of his week-long drunks*, Ed figured. Those were common enough.

The door slammed open.

Jimmy Dotson, a teenage punk Ed had little use for, stumbled in. A big rip ran through his shirt and blood coated his arm. He looked around the diner, confused and afraid.

Trouble. Ed thought about the rifle stashed under the counter, rarely used but loaded just the same.

"Shit," said Jimmy, looking at Ed. "You gotta lock the door."

"Something wrong, Jimmy?" said Ed, trying to get a read on the situation. "You hurt?"

Jimmy kept looking out the large window, between the big painted letters that said *Ed's* in reverse. "You gotta lock the doors. Where are the keys?"

Shit, thought Ed. *He's on something again. Hopefully he hasn't hurt anybody. And won't hurt anybody here.*

Ed cleared his throat. "Jimmy, don't you think you should have someone look at your arm?"

Jimmy let out a pained whine and pulled a pistol from his back pocket. He pointed it at Ed.

The diner fell quiet. A waitress behind Ed gasped and dropped a dish.

Jimmy shook as he spoke. "Please. Lock the fucking door right fucking now or I will shoot you and get the fucking keys my fucking self."

Ed stared at Jimmy. At the gun. His hand inched toward the rifle.

The gun rattled in Jimmy's shaking hand. "Please," he said, almost whispering.

At the edge of his vision, Ed saw movement outside. A bent form was shuffling toward the diner. Ed recognized the dirty jacket and battered cap. Old Timmins, no doubt coming for some post-drunk coffee. Timmins was a drunk, but he was a good man all around. And the customers were all good people too. And this drugged-up little shit was going to burst in and start waving a gun? Anger grew in Ed.

Jimmy looked over at the figure outside. He cried out. Ed seized the chance and snatched up the gun. He brought it out over the counter and fired.

The shot hit Jimmy in the shoulder. Blood spattered backward and Jimmy fell over. Ed's ears rang and the diner was silent.

Ed breathed out, his heart pounding. "Call an ambulance," he said to the waitress behind him.

The door jangled as Old Timmins pushed his way in.

"Picked a hell of a time to come up for air," said Ed, replacing the rifle under the counter. He reached for a clean coffee cup.

Timmins shuffled toward the counter. His head was down and he said nothing.

Ed placed the mug down as Timmins grew near. He reached for the coffee pot. Then it struck him as odd that Timmins hadn't reacted to the gunshot or the wounded punk on the floor.

Then Ed was screaming as Old Timmins sank half-rotten teeth into his arm.

One

Angela Land strode down a hallway in Lakewood Memorial Hospital. She moved with purpose through the florescent light and disinfectant smell. The small rural hospital had a few doctors, a few nurses and several nurse's aides. Angie was third on that list.

Her cell phone rang. She didn't stop or even slow down, sliding the phone from her smock and flipping her hair to one side.

She pressed the phone to her ear. "Hello?"

"Mom?"

Angie sighed. "What is it, Maylee? I'm at work."

"Brooke is being a bitch."

"She's the babysitter. Just do what she says."

Angie arrived at a large, dimly-lit laundry room. Several dryers were rumbling like hungry monsters. Her friend Freeda - also an aide - was folding sheets. Angie nodded and Freeda handed her one, grinning. Angie smiled and turned to leave. "And don't say bitch."

"Brooke said bitch," said Maylee.

Angie exhaled and walked back down the hall, holding the sheet. "Brooke's sixteen." The same age Angie had been when Maylee was born.

"I'm fourteen."

"Well, in two years you can start saying bitch. We'll have a party."

"Seriously?"

"No."

Maylee let out an exasperated groan. When Angie was in an honest mood, she knew those groans sounded just like her. "Don't you think fourteen is a little old for a babysitter?"

Angie counted the room numbers as they went by. 409, 410, 411 ... "Your brother's only twelve."

"Twelve's a little old, too."

"Look, Maylee, I just feel better if someone's there."

"I'm here, Mom. Don't you think I can handle it?"

"No one can handle everything."

"But you can?"

"I have to, Maylee, whether I want to or not. Now I have to go. Goodbye."

"Mom..." Maylee started, but Angie was already snapping the phone shut. She dropped it back into her pocket and reached room 425. Mr. Paulson.

"I'm back," she announced as she strode into the room and pushed the door shut with her foot. Old Mr. Paulson sat up in bed, a sheet crumpled around his ankles. The sheet was spattered with the remnants of his dinner.

"About goddamned time," he said. He spoke like he was spitting out something nasty. "I was freezing my nuts off."

Mr. Paulson's daughter sat in a chair next to his bed. Angie knew her to be 45, but her eyes looked older. Her name was Kristen.

"Now, Dad," she said, shaking her head. "It was you who dumped your food on the sheets."

"It tasted like half-digested turds," said Mr. Paulson. He glared at Kristen, then looked back to Angie. "How could you feed that to an old man? Especially a dying one?"

Angie smiled and pulled the dirty sheet from the bed. "Now, Mr. Paulson, I don't think you're dying."

Mr. Paulson snorted. "Well, you don't think much, then. I might look like the picture of health to a retard like you, but I ain't." He twisted around to slap the oxygen tank next to his bed. A tube ran from the tank to under his nose. "I've dragged one of these fuckers around for ten years."

Kristen exhaled. "Well, if you hadn't smoked for all those years..."

"Oh, monkey-clit." Mr. Paulson folded his arms and sat back. "Now you've got my daughter bitching at me."

Kristen smiled and shook her head. Angie dropped the dirty sheet and took the clean one in both hands. Kristen stood and held out her arms, offering to take the sheet. Angie shook her head and started unfolding.

Kristen sat. "Well, Dad, I just want to have you around as, long as possible."

Wow, thought Angie, *hell of a thing to wish on yourself.* She felt a little guilty for that, and turned her attention to the equipment sitting around the bed. If anything was obviously wrong, she'd have to report it to Nurse Ruby.

Then a scream came from somewhere down the hall. It was a woman, screaming loud and long. It sent a cold spike down Angie's back. All three of them turned to look at the door.

It swung open slowly.

A large man lumbered in. It was Sam Shuab, Kristen's husband. He was carrying paper cups of coffee.

"Man, some old chick's really squalling two rooms down," he said.

And then Angie remembered. "Oh, that's just Mrs. Reddens. She always yells when she has blood drawn." Angie had known that. Everyone on staff knew that. So why had it scared her? Something felt wrong tonight. Like something awful was sneaking up on her. She hadn't said anything to Maylee, but that was the main reason she'd insisted on a babysitter tonight. Someone else there. To keep watch. But for what?

"Poor old Mrs. Reddens," said Kristen.

Mr. Paulson snorted. "Poor old me, for having to listen to her. Moldy old twat's always shrieking at bingo, too. Enough goddamned noise to wake a corpse."

"I doubt she'd wake a corpse," said Kristen.

"Well, I'll know soon enough, first hand. Once the quacks here go cracking my chest open." He waved his arms to indicate the whole hospital.

"It's just for a pacemaker," said Angie. She stooped to pick up the dirty sheet. "It'll help with those chest pains."

"I'm sorry, miss," said Sam, handing Kristen a cup and sitting. "Are you a doctor?"

Angie's face flashed hot. "No."

"No, you're a hospital maid is what you are." He adjusted the glasses on his thick head. "Now go get us a damned doctor so we can talk sense to them."

"Sam," said Kristen sharply, looking at him.

"What?" said Sam. "He doesn't want the surgery. It's his call."

Kristen's face went dark. Angie smirked to herself. *You've done it now, asshole.*

"And quit fidgeting with your glasses," Kristen continued.

"I hate these stupid things," said Sam, taking them off and rubbing his eyes.

Angie bunched up the dirty sheet and did her best to smile. "Well, I'll go check on the doctor."

Sam and Mr. Paulson grunted something. Kristen smiled. Angie turned and left.

As soon as she was back in the hallway, her cell phone rang. She sighed, fished the phone out and answered.

"Mom?" came her son's voice.

"Dalton? What is it?"

"Maylee's not doing what Brooke says."

"Dalton, I don't have time..."

"And she keeps saying bitch."

* * *

"Bitch, bitch, bitch," said Maylee, skipping around the living room. She liked the way her hair, dyed the most screw-you black she could find, bounced with each step. How her mom hated that hair.

"I'm serious, Maylee," said Brooke, standing across the room with her arms folded. Brooke's hair was conservative and perfect. *I'm older*, her hair said. It pissed Maylee off. "Knock it off right now," said Brooke.

Maylee stopped skipping and crossed her arms, mocking Brooke. "But I don't know any better. I'm just a little baby."

"Well, you're certainly acting like a little baby."

Maylee rolled her eyes. "Oh, thank you, zinger queen. Your mom teach you that one?"

Brooke groaned and ran her hands through her hair. Maylee loved seeing that perfect hair falling out of place. "Why are you doing this, Maylee? Why can't we all just hang out until your mom comes home?"

"Because I don't need a babysitter, that's why!" Maylee turned and stomped toward her bedroom. She stopped when she heard Dalton's voice:

"And she keeps saying bitch."

She growled deep in her throat and pounded to the kitchen. She found Dalton at the table, phone to his ear.

Maylee sighed. "Are you telling on me, crotch-nostrils?"

Dalton grinned. "And now she's insulting me," he said into the phone.

Maylee snatched the phone and put it to her ear. "Mom, please. Why can't you just trust me?"

"You're just too young to be left alone all night," said Mom.

"But I know what I'm doing! I know better than to get knocked up like you did!"

As soon as the words left her mouth, Maylee knew she'd gone too far. She felt as though she'd hit her mom across the face. She wanted desperately to snatch the words back, but it was too late.

Mom was quiet for what seemed like minutes. Maylee finally spoke, her throat dry and cracking. "Mom..."

"Put Brooke on, please."

Brooke was already there, taking the phone from Maylee. "Ms. Land? I'm sorry." She nodded at whatever Mom was saying and straightened her hair. "Things really aren't as out of control as they sound."

Maylee bit the tip of her thumb and leaned back against the counter. Dalton stuck his tongue out at her. She kicked at him.

"Right," said Brooke into the phone. "No problem. See you later on. Bye."

"Wait," said Maylee, pushing herself up and reaching for the phone. But Brooke was hanging up and Maylee was too late. Again.

"I wanted to tell her I was sorry," said Maylee.

"Well, you'll get to talk to her later. I'll let you use my new cell phone."

Maylee reached for the phone. "No. Let me do it."

"Dammit, Maylee," Brooke snapped. "Back off or I'll tell your mom what you've been doing with your friend Stacy!"

Maylee looked at Brooke, mouth open. Dalton looked from Brooke to Maylee, then back to Brooke. He looked very amused. After a few seconds, Maylee gave Brooke a very dark look and sat back against the counter. "I just want to tell her I'm sorry," she said, almost a whisper.

Brooke sighed and drummed her fingers on the wall. Maylee leaned back and pouted. Dalton shifted uncomfortably.

Brooke looked around at the two of them and smoothed out her hair. "Okay." She picked up the phone. "I know I told your mom we might go out, but let's just order in. What do you two want on your pizza?"

Two

Angie walked back into the laundry room and dumped the dirty sheet into one of several large baskets. She put her hands on the base of her spine, then bent backward until a sore spot popped and felt relief. Around her, the washers rumbled and moaned.

"Troubles at home?" asked Freeda from behind the folding table. Freeda was chewing gum. She blew a little bubble and smiled.

Angie straightened and shrugged. She walked over to the table and grabbed a sheet to fold. "No new ones, if that's what you mean. Maylee just really chafes at having a babysitter."

"Well..." Freeda started. She looked at Angie, then back down at the sheets. Angie knew the look Freeda had just given her. It was Freeda's cautious look, the look she had when she was choosing her words carefully. "She is fourteen."

"Oh god." Angie shook her head, but smiled while she did it. "Not you too."

Freeda laughed. "I know, I know. They're your babies. And you've had Maylee since you were practically a baby yourself. But you have to start letting go a little."

Angie nodded and finished the sheet she was folding. She felt bad for being cold to Maylee. *Call home*, her mind nagged at her. *Tell her you're sorry*. "I know you're right, but..." She trailed off, putting the folded sheet on the stack Freeda had made. "Well, I don't know but what, just but something."

"I see," said Freeda, nodding as she finished the last sheet. She put it on the pile and raised an eyebrow at Angie. "*but* as in *butt out*."

Angie laughed. "No, no. Not like that." She helped Freeda straighten the stack, then they both headed for the door. Angie snapped off the light as they both left.

They walked down the hall quietly for a moment. "Speaking of butts," Angie said, "Sam Shuab..."

"Oh god, that prick." Freeda laughed. "You'd think Shuab Auto Sales was worth billions, the way he acts. What's he want?"

"A doctor," said Angie. "He's demanding one come talk to him."

They turned a corner and headed up a hallway toward the break room. Freeda frowned. "Mr. Paulson's refusing the surgery again?"

"Yep." Angie nodded, then thought for a moment. "Who's the doctor on duty, anyway?"

"Doctor Gordon."

"Oh great. Well, at least he and Sam should hit it off."

Freeda laughed. "I swear, if that little jackass was half the doctor he thought he was, he wouldn't have the late shift on a Thursday night."

Angie nodded. "This is true. He probably wouldn't even have this shift if he didn't have so many buddies on the board of directors."

They both turned another corner and almost collided with Nurse Ruby Meyer. Ruby had been headed the other direction and looked very annoyed at having been stopped. She was a tight-looking woman with a stern face and her hair pulled back taut.

"Where are you two going?" she said.

"Break room," said Angie as pleasantly as she could. Ruby made her nervous, but she refused to show it. "We're both pulling a double tonight, so I thought we'd take the chance to sit for a few minutes."

Ruby frowned for a tiny moment, then pushed past them. "Not yet, girls," she said as she walked up the hall. "I'll need everyone we can spare in ER. We've got a gunshot victim coming in. Someone who tried to rob Ed's."

Then she was gone around the corner. Angie and Freeda listened to the receding pat of Ruby's sneakers. Even with those sneakers, Angie could usually hear Ruby coming. Something was distracting her tonight. Something was wrong.

When Ruby was out of both sight and sound, Freeda turned to Angie. "What if we just don't show?"

Angie shook her head. "You know Ruby. That would be a bad idea." Then Angie felt a dread come over her. A feeling of something awful creeping up. *Call home*, she thought. *No, no time. Have to work.* "A very bad idea."

* * *

"I told you it was a bad idea," said Parker Welch as he whipped his groaning pickup into the parking lot of Lakewood Memorial. He ignored a speed bump and his muffler clattered in protest. His hunting cap began sliding off his long, unkempt hair and he tossed it off impatiently.

"The guy looked hurt, Park," said Morton Buck from the passenger seat. Park had known Moe for most of his thirty-five years, and Moe was constantly saying things like that. Stupidly nice things.

Moe rocked from side to side in rhythm with the truck. His teeth were clenched and he had one hand clamped over his left arm. Blood seeped from between his fingers.

"Fuck him," said Park. The truck's headlights bounced as he swung around, looking for a place to park. He found a spot near the emergency entrance and aimed for it. It was a handicapped spot, but Park ignored that. He was in a hurry. "That's what I said, and it's what you should have said too."

"Now, Park," said Moe, leaning to one side as the truck banked hard into the spot and stopped. "You can't ignore a fellow who's hurt."

Park let the engine run and stared across the front of the truck. He wondered what the hell had happened. The sun was going down on what was supposed to have been Parker's dying day. A nice, long-overdue hunting session with Moe, then home again to blow off the back of his head with a shotgun. Maybe he'd even feel the breeze against the back of his eyeballs before he winked out.

He hadn't told Moe, of course. Moe would have tried to stop him, showing the same stupid helpfulness that had gotten him bit.

"Well, he wasn't hurt, was he?" said Park, turning to him. "He was some crazy fucking asshole who bit you. Fucker was probably on meth or something."

He jerked the engine off and the truck shuddered in complaint. He realized he was still wearing his hunting gloves and he pulled them off, tossing them into a camouflage heap at Moe's feet. "Let's get inside."

Three

The emergency room was full. It was unusually busy for a Thursday night. But it wasn't just that. There was something unsettled in the atmosphere, something swirling in the air that Angie couldn't place.

"Wow," said Freeda next to her, looking around. "Things are bat-crap tonight."

And they were. Injured people were everywhere. A man with scratches on his face and a quickly bandaged leg. A woman in a torn and dirty dress, holding a cloth to deep red gashes on her arm. A young boy standing as his parents showed Nurse Paula gouges on his shoulder.

Paula looked over and nodded at Freeda. "Hey," she called, "come give me a hand."

Freeda turned to Angie. "Duty screams," she said, then rushed to the boy.

Angie stood in the middle of the room, taking it all in. There was definitely something wrong. The tone was off. The patients didn't look annoyed or embarrassed, the way most mildly injured people looked in the emergency room. They looked confused. And afraid.

That's it, thought Angie. *They look afraid.*
Call home.

"Hey, Anj," came a voice behind her.

She turned and saw Rick sitting at his dispatch desk. An old CB radio sat on the desk, waiting for the ambulance to call. Angie's eyes moved from the radio back to Rick. He was middle-aged, round and pleasant. Angie liked him. "What a night, huh?"

"No kidding." Angie nodded. "I hear we got a gunshot victim coming in."

"Yeah, someone tried to stick up Ed's. Can you believe it?" He looked around and rubbed his bristly goatee in a conspiratorial way, then leaned forward. "You know, that robber was not the only person to leave Ed's on a stretcher tonight. Only the coroner took the other one."

Angie's back went taut. The feeling returned. Something sneaking up. She stayed outwardly calm and leaned forward, raising an eyebrow.

Rick nodded. "Old Timmins."

"Oh god," said Angie. She'd seen Timmins here and there her whole life. He was a drunk, but a pleasant enough one. "Heart attack?"

"More like a stroke. He started biting people. Hard. As in drawing blood. By the time the cops and the ambulance showed up, he'd bit both Ed and some guy who tried to help. Even tried to bite a cop. Cop ended up shooting him."

"My god," said Angie.

Angie heard a stern cough from behind her. Rick made an "oops" face and quickly started looking busy. Angie turned to see Nurse Ruby.

"There's no time for chit-chat," Ruby said. "Please go straighten up the waiting room, Angela. We've had an unusual amount of traffic tonight."

No kidding, Angie thought. "Yes, ma'am." She gave a little parting smile to Rick and headed for the waiting room.

* * *

"I'm dying," said Dalton, clutching his stomach as he lay on the couch.

"You're not dying," said Brooke. She sat in Mom's chair with the TV remote in her hand. She hit the up button again and again, flipping through channels.

Maylee sat on the edge of another chair, across the room. "Can I have your stuff?"

Dalton said nothing, watching TV channels flash by. He slid his hand inside his open over-shirt and rested his palm on the t-shirt underneath.

"Hey, ass turtle!" said Maylee.

"What?" said Dalton, looking over.

"Can I have your stuff, since you're dying?"

Dalton shook his head and rubbed his stomach. The TV flipped past a news report, something about masses of people holding up traffic in a big city. "No, you'd better not. My things may be contaminated."

Maylee rolled her eyes. "I thought you were starving to death."

Dalton nodded. "I am starving, yes. But it may be a coincidence. I may be both starving *and* have a highly contagious disease."

Brooke chuckled as she clicked the remote. "You use lots of big words for a little brother."

Dalton beamed. "Mom says I'm smart."

"Sure," said Maylee. "To your face. To me, she says you're an ass turtle."

Dalton sat up and scowled at Maylee. "No she doesn't!"

Maylee held up her hands and sat back. "Hey, don't blame the messenger."

"I blame your ugly face," said Dalton. He stood, ignoring Maylee's quickly-flashed middle finger.

He frowned. "Is the pizza ever coming?"

The TV flipped past another news report, something about slow-moving mobs and random killings.

"Maybe food will save me." Dalton grabbed his stomach and made a big show of stumbling to the front window.

The usual view of their street greeted him outside. No car with a pizza sign.

He sighed and put his forehead on the glass. It felt cold. He gazed at a lit window in a house across the street. The light snapped out, sending an odd chill through Dalton. It was like the window had died.

A figure shuffled into view. It stumbled in from Dalton's right, headed to the left.

Dalton gasped and pulled away. The curtain fell back into place.

"What?" said Maylee from across the room. "The pizza?"

"No," said Dalton. He pushed the curtain over and squinted outside.

It was a man, stumbling slowly across the lawn. He looked like a man staggering just before falling down, only he never fell. He just kept taking one slow, herky-jerky step after another.

There was something wrong in the man's walk. *No*, Dalton thought. There was something wrong in the fact that the man was walking at all. Something said he shouldn't be walking. Shouldn't be doing anything.

The man jerked out from under a tree and into the moonlight, giving Dalton a clearer view. The man's head leaned all the way back, bouncing limply as he moved. His eyes were wide open, staring solidly at the moon.

Or at nothing.

"Dalton?" said Maylee, suddenly right behind him and breathing on his neck.

He jerked. "Crap, Maylee! Don't do that!" He turned to glare at her.

"What's your problem?" Maylee said, leaning to one side to look past him and out the window. "What's got you screeching like a little girl?"

"Nothing," said Dalton, embarrassed now. He turned back to gesture out the window. "There's just some weird guy on the lawn."

"Where? Oh, there he is." Maylee fell quiet as they both watched the man continue his *deeply wrong* walk across the lawn. A few seconds later, Dalton realized they were both holding their breath.

Then Brooke was behind them both. "For heaven's sake," she said. Both Dalton and Maylee jerked. Dalton heard Maylee gasp.

"It's just a drunk or something," said Brooke. "Go sit back down. The pizza should be here soon."

"Yeah," said Maylee, not sounding very convinced.

Dalton nodded and moved away from the window. He was blushing. He'd acted like a scared little kid. *Don't be such a baby*, he thought as he sat back down on the couch. *Look at Brooke, she's not afraid.*

But he noticed she stared out the window for a few extra seconds before turning away.

Four

Shambles, thought Angie as she stepped into the waiting room and looked around. Chairs were moved. Paper coffee cups were stacked everywhere. Magazines appeared to have been tossed around at random.

To Angie's left stood the reception desk, and Velma stood behind that. Velma had worked reception since Angie was a girl. Two men stood in front of the desk, talking to Velma. One clutched a wounded arm. Angie overheard that his name was Moe.

She moved past them and started cleaning. One of the men, the unhurt one, was complaining about having to wait to see the doctor. He sounded like a jackass.

She collected up several half-empty coffee cups and took them to a nearby trash can. Lukewarm coffee splashed on her hands as she dumped the cups inside. She cursed and wiped her hands on her smock. She looked around and saw at least three magazines nearby. She picked up two off of a nearby chair and went toward one lying on the floor just by a large window.

She knelt, picked up the magazine, then jerked back when something brushed the glass.

She stood, her heart skipping, and saw a woman pressed against the window. The woman moved feebly, writhing against the glass. Like she was trying to walk through it.

The poor thing's drunk, thought Angie as she tried to direct the woman to the doors. But the woman wasn't looking at her. The woman wasn't looking at anything, really. Her eyes were a milky yellow and her slowly opening and closing mouth revealed a swollen, gray tongue.

"Oh my god," Angie said, stepping back.

She heard movement behind her. Her back tightened and she spun around.

Dr. Gordon stood there. He was a short man with a lean face and a comb-over.

"Dr. Gordon," she said, breathing out. "Um, Nurse Ruby told me to clean up..."

He gave a little shake of his head to indicate he wasn't interested. "Ms. Land, I was just talking with Mr. Paulson's family."

"Oh, right," Angie said. "Mr. Paulson's saying he doesn't want..."

"Mr. Shuab told me you're trying to give medical advice."

Angie's cheeks tightened with heat. "No, sir, I was just..."

He shook his head again, dislodging his thin bangs. "You don't seem to realize what your duties are. And I must say I'm tired of complaints about your attitude."

Angie's first thought was to punch him. She'd never hit anyone before, but this little fucker had asked for it night after night. She needed this job, but damn it would be fun to...

Something bumped the glass behind her. She'd forgotten about the woman at the window.

"Sir, I think there's a woman who needs help," she said, turning to the window. The woman was gone. Only smears on the glass remained.

"Ms. Land!" Dr. Gordon shouted.

Angie spun back to see him fuming and readjusting his hair. "I'm afraid that's all I can take. If you can't even do the courtesy of looking at me while I'm talking to you, then..."

"Sir, please..."

"No, I'm sorry. I'm going to recommend the hospital board fire you."

"What?" Angie said. "You can't..."

"Now I hate to be a man who uses his connections, but I'm afraid I have no choice. If I were you, I'd start looking for other work."

He turned and walked toward the emergency room. Angie watched him go.

He couldn't.

Dr. Gordon pushed the emergency room doors open and walked through. The doors swung shut.

Angie blinked. She opened her mouth, then shut it.

He couldn't. He didn't have the authority.

But he did have the friends. A whole board-of-directors full.

So maybe he could after all.

Shambles, thought Angie as she sat down in the closest chair she could find, next to a soda machine. It hummed in her ear, but she barely noticed. She stared at the floor.

Call home.

Why not?

She took out her phone and started dialing.

* * *

Ten Minutes Earlier

"I don't believe this," said Park, drumming his fingers on the reception counter. "Can't you see how bad he's bleeding?"

"Be nice, Park," murmured Moe, clutching his arm. "It's not that bad."

"I understand, sir," said the fat old bitty behind the counter. "But we are unusually busy tonight. Just have a seat and the doctor will be with you as soon as possible."

"Great," said Park. "Just great." He paused to watch a woman in a hospital smock walk by. *Angie*, her name tag said. He turned back to the fat old bitty. "Thanks for the heaping help of jack fuck."

"Come on," said Moe, wincing slightly. "Let's sit."

Park grudgingly followed Moe to a chair and plopped down next to him. He ran a hand through his long hair, scratched at his stubble and absently watched "Angie" pick up magazines and cups around the room.

"Damn it," he muttered to no one in particular.

"Just try to relax," said Moe. Park turned back to see Moe looking at his red-stained palm. Moe put his hand back on his wound. "I'm the one who got bit."

Park sighed. "Yeah, I know. I'm just in a shitty mood."

Moe chuckled. "You're always in a shitty mood. You were born in a shitty mood. You wake up every morning in a shitty mood. And when you die, the doctors will tell your wife 'At least he died peacefully, in a shitty mood.'"

Park grunted. "Ex-wife. And I doubt she'd work up enough of a shit to show up." He hiked up one hip and fished around in his pocket for change. He cursed, switched hips and tried the other. This time he found some coins. "I saw a soda machine on the way in. You want one?"

"Don't know what I'd do with a soda machine," said Moe. "Doubt I could even carry it in my condition."

"Hey, it's the funniest fuck in fuck town," said Park. "You know what I mean, dipshit. Do you want a soda?"

"What I want is a beer," said Moe.

"You're in a hospital, Moe." Park looked around for the machine. Angie was talking to a balding man. She looked pissed.

Park looked back to Moe and smirked. "So you obviously can't have a fucking beer. What you can fucking have is a fucking soda." He rattled the coins in his hand. "Do you want one or not?"

Moe smirked back and shrugged. "Sure."

"Fine," said Park. He started to stand. The balding man walked past him on the way to the emergency room. Park sat back down and watched him go.

Park grunted. "Sure," he said loudly enough for the fat old bitty to hear. "He gets to go in."

"That was the doctor," said the fat old bitty.

"You shitting me?" said Park. "That was the doctor? Thanks for fucking telling him we got a hurt man here."

The fat old bitty sighed. "Please, sir, just be patient. I will let you know when he can see you."

Park snorted and stood. "Yeah, well, don't fucking hurt yourself rushing to help." He turned and walked to the soda machine.

Angie was sitting next to the machine. She stared at her cell phone as she slowly punched numbers in.

"Hey," said Park. "Not to interrupt whatever chat you're about to have, but my friend is hurt pretty bad. Are you people gonna get off your asses and do something?"

Angie looked up at him. She was mad, and Park was used to people being mad at him. But there was something else in her eyes. It took Park a second to recognize it.

Despair.

Then it was gone. "Sure," she said, snapping the phone shut. "But I'm just an aide. At least for tonight. I'll get you a nurse."

Five

Angie stepped back into the emergency room and looked around. Chaos. Every bed and chair was full. Aides scurried around, trying to attend to all the injured. *Tend, hell,* she thought. *It looks like it's all they can do to keep up.*

And all the injured had that same scared, confused look.

Dr. Gordon was gone. No nurses were in sight. Not even a free area the jackass' friend could sit.

She found Freeda, who was still tending to the wounded boy. The boy looked ill now, pale and sweating.

That's odd. He hasn't lost enough blood for that.

Freeda saw her and gave a weary smile.

Angie stepped over. "Where's Ruby? We got a guy in the waiting room who's bleeding pretty badly."

Freeda frowned. "Dunno. Outside smoking, I guess."

"Now? Great."

The dispatch radio sprang to life.

* * *

Ruby cursed and took a tight-lipped drag on her cigarette. She felt ridiculous, hiding outside in the dark to smoke. She considered walking down to the east wing of the building, where the ground sloped away from the hospital and no one would be able to see her from the windows. As far as she could remember, there weren't even any patients on that wing tonight. But that would be too ridiculous. She was a grown woman.

All the same, she hoped no one saw her. Her numerous failed attempts to quit smoking were hospital legend. And she was in no mood to catch any crap about failing again. If she couldn't smoke on a night as crazy as this, when could she?

She squinted out into the dark. The only light came from the door behind her. She couldn't see anything beyond a few feet.

She took another drag. She had to hurry. The ambulance would arrive soon, and there'd be no time for smoking then.

A shuffling sound came from the dark.

"Shit," she said, expecting an aide or even Dr. Gordon to appear and chastise her. But no one emerged.

She heard more shuffling. Then a slight groan.

Ruby frowned and took a third drag. More shuffling. Shaky, uneven footsteps. From more than two feet. Then another groan, from a different mouth.

"What the hell is going on?" she said, flicking the cigarette away and stepping into the dark.

After a few steps, she couldn't see a thing. The only light came from a few feet behind her. She heard moaning, grunting and the sounds of people stumbling.

"Is someone hurt?" she said.

Two arms landed on her shoulders. Cold hands clutched at her.

"Hey!" she said, twisting away from the arms. She was now standing facing the doorway and the only light. She heard movement next to her and took a step backward, further into the dark.

She backed into someone else. Cold arms closed clumsily around her breasts. The arms smelled awful.

"Get your hands off me!" Ruby yelled, angry now. She pulled the arms away from her. The skin on the arms felt wrong. Cold and spongy. She was wondering about that when a cold mouth closed on her ear.

She gasped as the mouth bit her ear off.

Pain shot through her head and she screamed, falling away from the arms as hot liquid ran down her cheek. She landed on her knees. She wanted to cover the wound, but it hurt too much to touch.

"What the hell is the matter with you?" Ruby shrieked into the darkness. She squinted but couldn't see anything.

A pair of legs ran into her back. Someone above her groaned and reached down, grabbing her hair. Ruby screamed and fought. The hands fumbled, a cold finger landing in the hole where her ear had been. The pain was so intense Ruby felt faint.

"Help!" Ruby yelled and wrenched away from the hands. She tried to stand but fell forward, still dizzy from pain. She landed on her stomach. Hands closed on her legs.

"Stop it!" Ruby yelled. A cold mouth closed on her calf. And bit. Teeth ground into her leg and tore a chunk free.

Ruby turned onto her back and kicked with her good leg. Something caught the leg and held tight. A second pair of hands closed on her head.

"Help!" Ruby screamed, cold fingers straying into her mouth. She fought and kicked, but the clammy hands held fast.

A third set of hands landed on her stomach. The hands fumbled with her clothes, pulling clumsily.

Ruby tried to scream but her mouth was full of cold fingers.

The hands on her stomach found skin. She heard groaning and the fingers dug into her stomach. Her shrieks were muffled as the hands pushed further into her. She felt her muscle and viscera tear. She felt bits of her being pulled out.

Then she felt nothing.

Six

The dispatch radio spat out static. Angie turned to look. Rick, still sitting at the dispatch desk, frowned. He leaned forward and clicked the microphone.

"Max? Pete?" he said.

Static. "Rick?" Static.

Rick clicked the microphone. "Where are you guys?"

"Shit!" Static. Garbled screaming. More static.

Click. "Guys?"

Angie started walking toward Rick's desk. Nurse Paula and the other aides turned to look. Even the patients turned to look.

Rick looked worried and clicked again. "Max? Pete? Come in."

Static. "Oh my god! Oh shit!" Static. Garbled screaming and groaning.

Angie reached Rick's back. She leaned forward to listen. Rick didn't notice. Angie peered out the glass ambulance entrance doors. She saw lights flicker outside.

"Guys?" Rick said, panic creeping into his voice.

"Oh god no!" Static. Screaming and gurgling. Wet choking sounds. Static.

Twin lights appeared outside. Approaching fast. Moving frantically side to side, but getting closer.

"Rick..." Angie started, surprised when her voice came out as a whisper.

"Max! Pete!" Rick screamed into the microphone. Only static replied. The lights were growing, huge and blaring into the emergency room.

"Rick!" Angie said, full volume now. "Oh shit."

"Guys!" Rick yelled into the microphone.

People behind her started screaming. The lights blared. An engine roared.

"Rick!" Angie yelled. She grabbed his collar and pulled him from the chair.

The glass doors and the wall surrounding them exploded. Angie was lost in heat and noise. She fell to one side, still holding Rick's hand. The dispatch desk flew past her, slamming into something. Angie couldn't tell what. All she knew was falling and the sounds of destruction.

Then, silence. Not real silence, just relative silence after the chaos. Angie blinked. She was lying on the emergency room floor. People around her cried and whimpered. She smelled smoke. No, an engine. An overheated engine.

Her head was turned away from Rick, but she could still feel his hand in hers. She tugged. The hand was oddly stuck in place.

"Rick?" she said, then turned her head to look.

One of Rick's eyes stared at her, wide and bulging. The other eye was gone. Lost along with most of his head, crushed flat under the wheel of the ambulance.

Angie screamed and let go, scrambling to her knees. Rick's head oozed blood and a thick, gray glop. Angie felt sick.

"Oh shit," came Freeda's voice from behind her.

Angie pushed down her vomit and stood. She looked around. Patients lined the walls, looking stunned. Aides stood with the patients. Angie barely knew any of them. They were newbies, and all clearly looked like they had quit the hospital the second the ambulance crashed through the wall.

Angie looked back at the ambulance. She spoke, her voice a hoarse whisper. "Freeda, where's Ruby?"

"Still out smoking," said Freeda from behind her.

Angie turned to look at Freeda. "Where's Paula?"

Freeda looked around, pale. She pointed, and Angie looked. The dispatch desk was smashed against the far wall. Nurse Paula was slumped over the desk's remains. Or, at least, the top half of her was.

Angie's stomach quivered as she turned back. "Shit."

She shook her head clear. "Okay then. Freeda, check the patients. I'll check the ambulance."

She moved to the ambulance - careful not to look at Rick's body or even *think* about it - and grabbed the driver's side door handle. She tugged but the door stayed shut. The window was cracked so badly she couldn't see in.

"Everyone stay calm," said Freeda behind her. "We'll find Nurse Ruby and Dr. Gordon and get everyone looked at."

Angie pulled on the door again, but it was locked or stuck. "Hello?" she called and knocked on the window. "Is everyone okay?"

She stepped onto the running board and peered between the cracks in the window. The front was empty. Something dark covered the driver's seat.

She hopped down and ran to the back. She was reaching for the door when something slammed against it from the inside.

Angie was so startled she stumbled backward, tripping over rubble from the destroyed wall. The patients began to squirm and mutter.

"Please stay calm," said Freeda to the patients. "Dr. Gordon will be here soon."

Angie looked at Freeda. "Call Nurse Ruby."

"What do you think I'm doing?" said Freeda, forcing a smile and holding her cell phone to her ear. "She's not answering."

Another *whump!* came from inside the ambulance. The door rattled. Angie turned back to face it.

"Hold on," she said to whomever was inside. "We're coming."

She grabbed the handle and opened the door.

First she saw blood. Red smeared everywhere across the silver of the ambulance. The thick copper smell of it was overwhelming.

Next she saw Pete, the driver. He was lying flat on the floor, splayed with his legs toward the driver's seat. The skin of his face was peeled back toward his scalp, revealing veins, muscle and two bulging eyes. Chunks of muscle were gone, his skull showing through underneath.

Then she saw Jimmy, the gunshot victim. The kid who'd tried to stick up Ed's. He sat on the floor of the ambulance, with Max - the paramedic - across his lap. Most of Max's throat was gone. Blood covered Jimmy's lap. Jimmy reached into Max's throat and pulled out a handful of stringy connective tissue. He shoved it into his mouth and chewed.

Jimmy saw Angie and dropped Max. He groaned and reached for her.

Angie screamed and slammed the door. She could hear Jimmy scratching from the inside. The patients gasped.

"Ms. Land!" came Dr. Gordon's voice from across the room. Jimmy pushed against the door.

Dr. Gordon strode quickly to the ambulance. "I knew you were lax in your duties, but slamming doors on the injured?"

"Dr. Gordon, wait..." said Angie, struggling to hold the door shut. Jimmy groaned.

Dr. Gordon stepped up next to her. "You were damned near fired before. You're damned fired now."

He pushed her aside and pulled on the door.

Jimmy fell forward as the door swung open. He clutched hold of Dr. Gordon's stomach.

"Whoa, there," said Dr. Gordon. "Don't strain yourse..." Then he screamed as Jimmy bit into his stomach.

Angie screamed and pulled Dr. Gordon back. Jimmy held tight and fell out of the ambulance, his face buried in Dr. Gordon's stomach. Blood ran past Jimmy's head and onto the floor.

"Freeda!" yelled Angie. "Help!" She tugged on Dr. Gordon. But Jimmy would not come free. Jimmy moaned ecstatically and pushed his face further into Dr. Gordon. His head disappeared into Dr. Gordon's stomach.

Dr. Gordon shrieked and bucked. Blood ran from his nose and mouth. Freeda reached them and grabbed hold of Dr. Gordon's shoulders. Jimmy groaned, muffled from within Dr. Gordon's innards.

Dr. Gordon stopped shrieking and his head lolled back. Jimmy tried to push himself deeper inside. Angie put a foot on Jimmy's torso.

"Pull!" she yelled and both she and Freeda yanked back. Jimmy's head came free of Dr. Gordon with a horrible wet sound.

Angie and Freeda fell back with Dr. Gordon. Angie landed on her tail bone and pain shot through her. Freeda landed next to her. Dr. Gordon was splayed across both their laps.

Jimmy knelt where he had fallen, chewing on something. His face and shoulders were covered in blood and meat. Thick red cords ran from his mouth to Dr. Gordon's ruined abdomen. Angie blinked and realized they were intestines.

Jimmy moaned and chewed.

The patients screamed and ran in all directions.

Most of the patients rushed out the door to the waiting room. The other aides went with them. They quickly crowded together and blocked the way out. Those who were left started screaming and pulling at each other, trying to get through.

Angie sat stupefied, staring at Jimmy eating Dr. Gordon's intestines. Her tail bone smarted but she barely registered the pain.

Freeda scrambled away from Dr. Gordon's body and stood. "Come on," she said. "Let's go."

Angie shook her head clear. "No."

"What? Are you crazy?"

Angie stood, doing her best to ease Dr. Gordon's body down. "We can't leave him here with the patients." She pointed at Jimmy, who ignored them and chewed. "He can get to the patient rooms from here. Hell, he can get to the maternity ward."

People behind her screamed and clawed at each other.

Freeda frowned. "Shit. The Wilson triplets."

Angie nodded and wiped sweat from her face.

Freeda looked at Jimmy, then back at her. "He's fucking eating him."

"I know," said Angie. "Try not to look."

The crowd behind them broke through the jam and they poured out of the room.

Freeda sighed. "You're crazy."

"Someone has to do something."

Jimmy groaned and looked at Freeda. He dropped the intestines and crawled toward her.

"Oh shit," said Freeda. "This is crazy." She backed away, hiding behind Angie.

Jimmy slowly climbed to his feet. He stared at Angie and Freeda through clouded eyes. Blood ran from his mouth.

"Okay," said Angie, stepping back. "Jimmy? Try to calm down. I think you're on something very bad. Just try to rest, okay?"

Jimmy gurgled through the blood in his mouth and reached for them. Freeda screamed and jumped back. Angie stepped the other way. Jimmy followed Freeda.

"Anj..." said Freeda, sounding very nervous.

"Jimmy?" said Angie. "You've been in a very bad accident. I really think you should lie down."

Jimmy grabbed at Freeda. Freeda ducked out of the way but he caught hold of her smock.

"Hey!" said Angie, shoving Jimmy.

He stumbled away from Freeda and let go. Freeda ran off to one side. Jimmy blinked his fogged eyes and gargled in blood.

Finally his attention fell on Angie.

He groaned and came at her.

"Jimmy, stop it," said Angie, backing away, toward the ambulance.

Jimmy kept coming.

"Stop it, Jimmy!" Angie said, trying to sound forceful.

Her back met the ambulance. Jimmy drew close.

Freeda yelled and smacked Jimmy across the back of the head with something heavy. As Jimmy fell, Angie saw it was a fire extinguisher.

"Shit," said Freeda, looking at the extinguisher and then at Angie.

"Thanks," said Angie. "Now let's call the cops."

Jimmy grunted and started climbing to his feet.

"Wow," said Freeda, looking down.

Angie stepped over to Freeda. "Give me that," she said, taking the fire extinguisher.

"Jimmy?" she said. "Please stay down. We don't want to hurt you any more."

Jimmy finished standing.

"How hard did you hit him?" asked Angie.

"Hard," said Freeda.

"Shit," said Angie. Jimmy groaned and reached for her, teeth gnashing.

Angie screamed and swung the extinguisher at his head. His head snapped back and he fell over backward.

"Damn it, Jimmy," said Angie, shaking a little. "Don't make me hurt you any more."

Jimmy stirred and started to stand.

"Oh shit," said Freeda.

"Jimmy, please," said Angie. "You have to stop." She thought about what she'd heard about Old Timmins. How he hadn't stopped until a cop shot him.

Jimmy got to his feet and grabbed Angie. He pulled her toward himself, his mouth strained open to bite.

"Anj!" yelled Freeda.

Angie pulled free and swung the fire extinguisher at the side of Jimmy's head. Fear and adrenaline fueled the blow. She almost strained her back from the force.

Jimmy's head snapped to one side. A thin line appeared on the opposite side of his neck. Dark blood seeped out.

"Oh shit," said Angie. "I'm sorry. You're hurt bad, Jimmy. Please stop."

Jimmy moaned and reached for Angie again. His head hung limply to one side. His mouth chewed at the air.

"Goddammit, Jimmy!" yelled Angie and swung the extinguisher the other way. Jimmy's head whipped to the other side. The skin on his neck split and with a sloppy cracking noise his head came free.

Both Angie and Freeda screamed as Jimmy's head fell to the floor and bounced. Jimmy's body slumped, blood seeping from its open neck.

"Oh shit, you killed him!" said Freeda, sounding near crying.

"I know!" said Angie, dropping the extinguisher. "But he wouldn't stop! He wouldn't fucking stop!"

Then she noticed something.

Jimmy's head lay on its cheek against the emergency room floor. But Jimmy's mouth was still moving. His cloudy eyes looked around and his teeth continued to gnash at nothing. His eyes found Angie and he ground his teeth at her.

"Okay," said Angie. "Now I think we should go."

Angie and Freeda ran for the doors to the waiting room, just as a crowd of people rushed in. It was the patients and aides who'd run out before. They were screaming.

They ran blindly past Angie and Freeda. Two men burst in after them. Angie recognized them as the jackass and his hurt buddy.

"We got problems," said the jackass.

Seven

Fifteen Minutes Earlier

"Dammit," said Park as he paced the waiting room. "How in the fuck could it possibly take this long?"

Moe was still grasping his arm. "It's only been a few minutes."

"Few minutes of pissing me off." Park looked back to the emergency room doors and scowled. The fat old bitty at the reception desk glanced at him, then looked down. Park snorted and turned to pace the other way.

He took one step.

An enormous crash came from the emergency room.

Park whipped back around. "Shit! What the fuck was that?"

The fat old bitty rushed to the doors. "I'll check. Stay here." She pushed her way into the emergency room and the doors swung shut behind her.

Park watched her go, then turned to pace some more. He heard Moe stand and he turned back.

Moe frowned at the doors. "What do you think's going on, Park?"

Park shrugged. "Fuck if I know. Hopefully it clears a spot in there." He looked at the doors for a second, then sighed. "I guess let's see."

He walked to the doors and Moe followed. He pushed the doors open a crack and peered inside. Moe looked over his shoulder.

The emergency room was in shambles. An ambulance sat in the middle of the room. A large hole was ripped in one wall. Angie, the aide Park had talked to, was running to the ambulance.

"Damn," said Moe. "Maybe we should help."

"Fuck that shit," said Park. "We need to get you to another hospital." He stepped back from the door and turned to Moe.

Moe frowned. "But the nearest hospital is hours away."

Park nodded back toward the emergency room. "I think here will take longer."

Moe winced and looked pale. "Okay, but let's hurry. I don't feel so good."

"Sure thing," said Park. They both went toward the exit doors.

And stopped when they reached them.

Outside in the parking lot, two girls in cheerleader uniforms were ripping a grown man apart.

The man stood screaming as the girls tugged at him from either side. One ripped a chunk of his chest free and stuck the bloody meat into her mouth and chewed. Blood ran down her chin and she looked toward the hospital. And at Park.

Behind the cheerleaders, a crowd of people slowly drew near.

"Shit," said Park.

A screaming mob of people burst from the emergency room. Park had less than a second to look back before the mob swept him and Moe outside.

"What the fuck?" yelled Park. He grabbed Moe and yanked him to one side of the parking lot, out of the way of the rushing mob.

The front of the mob ran into the crowd that was slowly coming the other way.

The mob started screaming.

Park stared as he watched one group of people *eat* the other.

"Park..." said Moe.

"Yeah," said Park, still staring.

An old man missing one eye bit into a young girl's cheek. He pulled away a long strip of flesh and chewed. The young girl shrieked.

"They're eating them," finished Park.

"I think we should go back inside," said Moe.

"Yeah."

They turned and tried to push their way back into the hospital. The back end of the mob was still trying to push its way out. They were screaming about whatever had sent them running from the emergency room. The front of the mob was screaming as the approaching crowd bit and ripped at them. The whole world was full of screams.

Moe stopped in the middle of the mob. He swayed back and forth. "Park..."

"Not now!" said Park, grabbing Moe's collar and pulling him toward the doors.

"I don't feel so good," said Moe.

"Turn around you dumb motherfuckers!" yelled Park as he forced his way through the mob.

"Park!" Moe screamed.

Park turned back. One of the crazy cannibals - a fat woman in a rotting dress - had hold of Moe and was pulling him down to the asphalt. Her mouth was open and she was straining to bite.

"Shit!" yelled Park. Moe fell out of sight, lost in the dark of the parking lot and the shadows of the surrounding mob. "Moe!"

People pressed around Park. Moe's hand slipped from his grasp. Into darkness.

"Damn it," said Park, fishing out his lighter. He shoved people aside and flicked the lighter on, bending down to where he had last seen Moe.

Moe was struggling with the fat woman, who was doing her best to bite but hadn't succeeded. The woman pulled away from Park's lighter, hissing at the flame and letting go of Moe.

Park grabbed Moe's hand and pulled him up. "Come on!" He snapped the lighter off and dropped it back in his pocket.

The woman grabbed for Moe again.

"Fuck off!" yelled Park, punching the woman in the face. Her head snapped back, then slowly righted as if nothing had happened. She groaned at them.

Park looked around. The crazies were closer. They were working their way through the mob, drawing nearer to the doors. Blood was everywhere. The thick smell of it stung Park's nose.

Finally, the remaining mob behind Park realized what was happening. They screamed and changed direction, running back into the hospital. Park almost fell backward at the sudden shift.

"Hurry!" he yelled, pulling Moe toward the hospital. The crazy woman grabbed at them but missed.

Park and Moe spilled back into the waiting room.

"Shit fuck hell," Park muttered, looking around. The mob was rushing back into the emergency room. Park saw nowhere else to go, so he followed, pulling Moe with him.

As they entered, he almost collided with Angie and some other aide.

"We got problems," he said.

Eight

Brooke sighed as she clicked the TV remote. Why couldn't she just find something mindless the three of them could watch, just to pass the time?

The doorbell rang.

Dalton sat up on the couch. "Pizza!"

"Stay put," said Brooke, standing and setting the remote down. "I'll get it."

She walked to the front door and opened it. A teenage boy stood there, holding a pizza box. His hat said *Pizza Plaza*.

"Hey," said Brooke, unzipping her purse.

"Hi," said the boy, looking up and down the street. "There something going on around here tonight?"

"Hmmm?" said Brooke, half-listening as she rooted around for cash.

"Got a lot of weirdos wandering around tonight," said the boy, looking back at her.

"Who knows," said Brooke, finding a twenty and looking back up at the boy. "Got too much on my mind tonight, watching these two."

"Yeah." The boy tried a little laugh. "Anyway, $18.50."

And an old woman came up and bit the boy's neck. He gasped in surprise. Blood shot out of his throat and onto Brooke's shirt. Huge drops of it fell on the pizza box.

Brooke screamed and slammed the door.

Shock gave way to guilt and she opened the door to help.

"What's going on?" said Dalton behind her.

The boy was now being dragged down the street by two old ladies. The first one chewed on his neck as he struggled weakly. The second old lady grabbed one of his arms and brought his hand to her mouth. She bit into the top and tore off a huge flap of skin, exposing bone and muscle. The boy tried to scream and gargled in his own blood.

"Oh shit," said Brooke, staring.

"Oooh," said Maylee from across the room. "Big girl gets to cuss."

"Shut the fuck up, Maylee," said Brooke, shutting the door and locking it. She stepped away from the door, fishing into her purse for her cell phone. She had to call the cops.

"Nice," said Maylee, getting up and stomping to the door. "Don't tell me what to do, bitch."

She opened the door and screamed.

A man in a muddy suit grabbed her and pulled her out the door.

"Maylee!" yelled Dalton, racing outside.

"Damn it!" yelled Brooke, following.

Outside, Maylee was struggling with the man. He was trying to bite her but Maylee was barely holding him off. Two teenagers were approaching. One had half his face missing.

Dalton grabbed one of Maylee's shoulders. Brooke grabbed the other. The man pulled Maylee toward him. The teenagers drew near.

Maylee screamed and kicked the man in the face. He fell back and let go.

Dalton and Brooke pulled Maylee inside as the teenagers grabbed for them. Dalton shut the door and locked it.

"What the fuck!" shrieked Maylee.

"Don't open the door!" said Brooke.

"No shit, really?" said Maylee, pacing. "What the hell is going on?"

"I don't know," said Brooke, looking for her phone again.

Dalton was looking out the large front window. "They're eating the pizza guy."

"You mean the pizza," said Maylee.

"No," said Brooke, "he means the pizza guy."

Maylee went to the window and looked. "Oh shit."

"The cops aren't answering," said Brooke, holding her cell phone to her ear. "Why the hell aren't they answering?"

Maylee and Dalton turned to look at Brooke. Maylee walked over. "Let me try."

"I know how to dial, Maylee," said Brooke.

The window crashed in. Four arms grabbed Dalton and pulled him outside.

"Fuck!" yelled Maylee, running and jumping out the window.

"Damn it!" yelled Brooke. "I'm in charge here! Stay inside!"

She ran to the window. Maylee was pulling Dalton away from the two teenagers. Brooke climbed out to help. One of the old ladies, face covered in the pizza boy's blood, grabbed her.

The smell from the woman was awful. Her skin was clammy and cold. Brooke's grandfather had died two years ago. Brooke had touched him in the coffin. His skin then felt like the old woman's now. The woman hissed at her and leaned in to bite.

Maylee's foot slammed into the woman's head. The old woman fell over and Brooke scrambled away.

"Hitting them in the head seems to help," said Maylee.

"Back in the house," said Brooke. The old woman was getting up. The teenagers were closing in. The man with the muddy suit was coming up from one side.

She helped Dalton back in the window. Maylee climbed in and Brooke followed. The group of crazy attackers was approaching the window.

"We need to block the window," said Maylee.

"Here," said Brooke. "Help me." She grabbed hold of the couch and pushed it toward the window. Maylee and Dalton joined her. The three of them tipped the couch up onto its side, against the window. The crazies outside pushed at it.

The three of them stepped back and looked at the couch. "That's not gonna hold long," said Dalton.

The couch started falling forward. Brooke caught it. Maylee and Dalton each grabbed a side. Arms reached past the couch and grabbed at them. One of the arms was missing most of its flesh.

"This isn't working!" yelled Maylee.

"Shit!" said Brooke. "Run!"

They ran away from the couch, across the living room and into the hall. The couch thumped to the floor behind them.

"Get to the back door!" said Brooke.

"Wow, no shit?" said Maylee.

"Not now, Maylee!" yelled Brooke.

They ran into the kitchen. They stopped, sneakers squeaking on the linoleum.

A man in an old-fashioned suit was there, stumbling toward them. His skin was dry and taut against his skull. Thin white hair barely hung from his scalp.

Brooke blinked.

His eyes were gone.

He groaned at them.

Dalton screamed from behind Brooke. The back door that led out from the kitchen slammed open. A large woman missing an arm staggered in.

"Come on!" yelled Maylee from behind Brooke. "We can get out my bedroom window!"

Brooke shook her head clear.

"Yeah," she said. The three of them ran from the kitchen.

They made it to Maylee's bedroom. Maylee climbed onto the bed and knelt by her window. She undid the lock and pushed the window up.

"Come on!" she said, looking back at Brooke and Dalton.

A withered hand reached inside and grabbed Maylee's hair.

"Maylee!" Dalton screamed and rushed to the bed. Brooke followed.

Dalton grabbed the arm and tugged. Brooke grabbed the arm and tried to push it out the window.

Maylee frantically tugged at the fingers in her hair. Brooke changed tactics and tried to help. She did her best to pull the fingers from Maylee's hair. Maylee grunted and squirmed. Brooke could hear panic in her voice.

Dalton yelled and leaned backward, pulling at the arm as hard as he could. With a sloppy tearing noise a huge sheet of skin came free of the arm. He screamed and dropped the skin.

The arm showed no reaction. It pulled Maylee toward the window.

Brooke let go and stood on the bed. She grabbed the window and slammed it down on the arm.

The arm didn't flinch.

"Shit," she said, pulling the window back up.

The arm pulled Maylee closer to the window. Maylee screamed.

Brooke slammed the window down again. It bounced off the arm, snapping back up a few inches.

The arm kept pulling Maylee steadily toward the window. Maylee kicked at the bed, dragging dirt across the sheets.

"Goddamn it!" yelled Brooke, pulling the window up.

"Look out!" screamed Maylee, her head drawing near to the windowsill.

Brooke screamed and slammed the window down as hard as she could. It hit the arm on the wrist, inches away from Maylee's head.

The wrist snapped and the hand tore free. Maylee scrambled up and off the bed. She screamed with disgust as she pulled the hand out of her hair and dropped it.

"What the fuck!" she shrieked.

"There's no blood," said Dalton.

Brooke and Maylee looked at the severed hand on the floor. There was no blood anywhere.

"What the fuck!" Maylee repeated. "Why the fuck isn't there any blood?"

Groans came from the living room and kitchen.

"Shit," said Brooke. "We need to get to a room they can't get in."

"The bathroom," said Dalton. "There's no windows."

Brooke nodded. "Hurry."

She led them to the hallway. A crash came from the living room and they stopped to look. Three crazies were climbing over the fallen couch. A fourth was stepping onto the TV, which had apparently just fallen.

Groaning came from Brooke's side. Cold hands grabbed her and Dalton screamed. The eyeless man from the kitchen had her.

Brooke screamed and tried to push the man away. He clacked his rotten teeth together, inches away from biting her.

"Let her go!" yelled Dalton, kicking the man in the side.

Maylee ran back into her bedroom.

"Maylee!" yelled Brooke, struggling with the man. "We have to stay together!"

The four crazies in the living room were getting closer.

"Let her go!" Dalton repeated, kicking the man again.

Maylee ran back into the hallway, holding an aluminum baseball bat. Screeching, she brought the bat down on the man's head. The man's skull caved, crumpling his forehead into a frown. The man let go.

"See!" yelled Maylee. "The head!"

Brooke pushed the man back into the kitchen. She briefly noticed the woman missing an arm - the one who'd followed the man into the kitchen - was gone.

"Into the bathroom," she said. "Hurry!"

They rushed further down the hallway, then banked left in the bathroom. Brooke turned, let Maylee and Dalton past her, and shut the door. Brooke's sweating hands fumbled as she pushed the handle in and turned it, locking the door.

Maylee sat back against the sink, clutching the bat. Dried skin caked the top of it. Dalton leaned against the toilet.

For a second they all stared at each other, panting.

Then the shower curtain collapsed at them. It draped Brooke, knocking her to the floor. Brooke felt the weight of a person atop her, writhing against the curtain that separated them. Groaning breath hit where the curtain stretched against Brooke's cheek. The breath smelled foul but had no heat. It was cold.

Brooke screamed and pushed up. A hand grabbed at her and teeth ground against the curtain.

Brooke heard Dalton and Maylee screaming. The person atop her shook as something repeatedly struck them. *Maylee's bat,* Brook realized.

"Where the hell did she come from?" yelled Maylee.

"I recognize her from the kitchen!" yelled Dalton. "She must have wandered to the bathroom while we were in your bedroom."

"Get her off of me!" shrieked Brooke.

Brooke heard Maylee and Dalton scrambling to grab hold of the woman. A few seconds later, her weight shifted upward.

Brooke scrambled out from under the curtain. Her attacker, the large woman missing an arm, was struggling in Dalton's and Maylee's grip. She bit at all three of them, missing but coming close.

"Open the door!" yelled Maylee.

"Are you crazy?" said Brooke, panting. "They're out there..."

"We can't keep her in here!" yelled Maylee.

Brooke swallowed. Maylee was right.

Brooke turned, braced herself, and unlocked the door.

She opened it. The eyeless man stood there, reaching for them. Other crazies reached around the door frame.

"Duck!" yelled Maylee.

Brooke did.

Maylee and Dalton shoved the lady forward. She stumbled, tripped over Brooke and fell out the door. She knocked the eyeless man over and they both fell into the hallway.

Brooke stood and slammed the door. She locked it as fast as her shaking hands would allow.

"Shit," said Maylee.

"Is everyone okay?" said Brooke. She turned to put her back to the door. Groaning and scratching came from the other side.

Dalton and Maylee nodded.

Brooke nodded in reply and slid down to sit on the floor. She put one foot against the side of the toilet, bracing the door with her body.

"What do we do now?" said Dalton.

"Now," said Brooke, fishing around in her pockets. "We call the cops again."

Dalton nodded. Brooke felt in her pockets more frantically, panic growing. "My phone."

"What?" said Maylee.

Brooke sighed and put her forehead in her palms. "My cell phone. I must have dropped it in the living room."

Maylee and Dalton stared at her.

Dalton swallowed. "And the house phone is in the kitchen."

Brooke nodded and sighed, looking around the windowless room.

"Shit."

And groaning and scratching came from behind the one and only door.

Nine

"We got problems," said the jackass in the hunting jacket. His hurt friend - was his name Moe? - was pale and sweating behind him.

Angie nodded. "Yeah. I just knocked someone's head off with a fire extinguisher. I'm going to get the cops."

Behind her, Freeda made a worried noise. "The head's still moving."

Angie sighed. "Don't look at it, Freeda."

"That doesn't stop it moving."

"Stops you talking about it."

Moe swayed back and forth slightly. "Park, I feel bad..."

The jackass - apparently named Park - frowned at Angie and Freeda. "I give such a shit about everything you're saying, I really do. But you ain't getting out that way."

He pushed the doors to the waiting room open. Looking past him, Angie could see a few patients struggling with a crowd that was slowly pushing its way into the waiting room. One member of the crowd - a teenager with a religious t-shirt - bit into the face of a patient - an elderly woman with a walker. The woman screamed as blood shot out onto the teenager's face.

Angie heard movement behind her. She turned to see someone slowly coming through the hole the ambulance had made.

It was an overweight man, half in the room and half out. He blinked at the floor as he tried over and over again to pull himself into the room. He reached into the room with one hand. The other arm was hidden outside, behind the edge of the hole.

"Sir?" Angie started to say.

The man groaned and lurched the rest of the way into the room. He had no other arm. He had a stump, fresh and bloody.

Movement came from the floor. Angie looked down. Dr. Gordon was getting up. He straightened and his wet guts spilled out onto the floor. He took a step toward Angie and the others, his foot clumsily squishing on a loop of his own intestines.

Angie opened her mouth to react, then noise came from the ambulance. Max and Pete crawled out of the open back doors. Wet cords dangled from Max's open throat, bouncing limply against his gore-soaked chest as he staggered. Pete groaned. The flap of skin that had been Pete's face flapped slowly with each step he took. Thick dark blood ran down his neck and shoulders.

Angie bit her lip. "Is that happening?"

"Yeah," said Freeda.

"Shit," said Angie.

"We need to go," said Park. Moaning grew from the waiting room.

Angie nodded. "There's two other side exits. Follow me." They ran.

Angie led them down the hall to the nurse's station at the center of the hospital. It consisted of a long desk with two computers and three chairs, abandoned and empty.

Park entered last, helping Moe along with him. "Which way?" he said.

"One second," said Angie. She moved to the door they had just come through. It was solid glass with locks at the top and bottom. She closed the door and locked it.

"These doors are reinforced glass," she said. "This way they can't follow us or get to the patient rooms."

"I'm so glad I know that," said Park, adjusting Moe's weight on his arm. "Which fucking way?"

Angie turned, taking in the three other hallways that went off from the nurse's station. She chose one.

"Here," she said, pushing past Freeda and heading down the hall. The others followed.

They rushed past several patient rooms. Patients sat up in their beds, looking confused and worried.

"Is something wrong?" said one, an older woman with several IVs.

"Everything's fine," yelled Angie as she ran by. "Everyone just stay calm. And whatever you do, don't open the locked door at the nurse's station."

Park snorted. Angie cast a glare back at him.

"As soon as we get out of here," she said, "we'll call the cops to come rescue the patients."

"Yeah," said Park. "I'll get right on that."

They were halfway to the exit door when a group of crazies burst in.

"Shit!" yelled Angie, stopping.

"Where the fuck are they all coming from?" said Park.

Screams came from all directions. From the patient rooms. Crashing glass echoed through the hallway.

"The windows!" said Freeda.

"Oh god, no!" yelled Angie.

"We gotta move," yelled Park, already rushing Moe back the way they had come.

"We have to save the patients!" said Angie.

"There's too many of those crazies," said Freeda. "We have to run!"

Angie looked at Freeda. Behind Freeda, Park was fighting off a crazy. Blood ran from the crazy into the patient room it had come from. Patients were screaming. Crazies were coming up the hall from behind.

Angie swallowed. "Shit. Let's go."

She and Freeda ran up the hall. Angie stopped halfway to Park and stared into a patient room. The older lady with multiple IVs was splayed across her bed, head facing the door. Her head hung back over the edge of the mattress, empty eyes staring at Angie. A toddler was atop her. He had the woman's gown lifted up and was chewing on one of her breasts. He tore free a hunk of skin, fat and blood. He chewed and looked at Angie.

"Angie!" came Freeda's voice from up the hall.

Angie turned to look. Freeda was struggling to pull a crazy from Park. The crazy was snapping its teeth inches away from Park's cheek. A second crazy was coming up behind Moe.

Angie ran to help. She reached Moe first and pulled him away from the crazy's reach. Moe was covered in sweat.

Moe blinked slowly, looking very confused.

"Sir?" said Angie, feeling his head. It was very hot. "Are you alright?"

"Shit!" yelled Park. Angie turned to look. The crazy, a bodybuilder with huge muscles and a hole where his nose had been, was close to biting into Park's neck. Freeda was holding the bodybuilder back, pulling on his arm so hard she was leaning backward. It didn't look like she could hold him much longer.

Angie grabbed Park and pulled the other way.

"Goddamit, this fucker's strong!" said Park.

And he was. The crazy inched closer. Soon his teeth would find skin.

"For fuck's sake," came Moe's thick, slightly slurred voice. Moe reached down and grabbed one of the crazy's legs. He pulled and the crazy toppled over, letting go of Park.

They all looked at the crazy for a second, watching it writhe and groan. It was struggling to get up.

"Why didn't we think of that?" said Freeda.

Groans came from all around. The screams of the patients were fading.

"We gotta get," said Park.

"Yeah," said Angie. "Come on."

They ran back toward the nurse's station, Angie willing herself not to look in the patient rooms. *We'll call the cops*, she told herself. *We'll call the cops and they'll rescue the rest of the patients.*

They reached the nurse's station. Angie turned and shut the glass door to block the way they had come.

"Those nut jobs can come right through glass!" said Park.

"I told you," said Angie as she locked the top and bottom of the door. "These are reinforced glass. They're stronger than the windows."

Moe threw up on the floor.

"Fuck!" yelled Park.

"I'm okay," said Moe, swaying and wiping his mouth.

"Fuck you are," said Park.

"Come on," said Angie. "This way."

Angie leading the way, they rushed down another hallway. Heading for another exit door at the end of it. Patients looked at them as they passed.

"If anyone has a phone," yelled Angie, "call the cops! Stay in your rooms and don't open the nurse's station..."

Crazies burst in the door at the end of the hall.

Angie skidded to a halt. "No!"

Glass crashed all up and down the hallway. Patients shrieked.

"No!" Angie screamed.

"They're surrounding the hospital!" yelled Freeda.

"Everyone out of your rooms!" yelled Angie. But she knew from the screams it was too late.

She looked back toward the nurse's station. Park was pulling Moe that way as fast as he could. Freeda was staring at Angie.

"Come on!" said Freeda. "We have to go!"

"The patients..." Angie started, weakly.

"It's too late," said Freeda.

Then a little boy burst from a patient room. He shrieked and sobbed but looked unhurt. He nearly collided with Angie.

"Whoa, hey," said Angie, trying to sound soothing despite the chaos around. She put a hand on the boy's shoulder and looked at him. She did her best to ignore the approaching crazies behind him. "Are you okay?"

"My mom!" yelled the boy. "They're eating!"

"Who..." Angie started, then Freeda screamed behind her.

Angie let go of the boy and turned. A crazy had snuck up behind Freeda. He looked like a truck driver, complete with mutton chops. One of his eyes dangled from its optic nerve, bouncing off his cheek as he struggled with Freeda.

"Freeda!" yelled Angie, moving to help. Then the little boy screamed. Angie turned to see a woman wearing a hospital gown closing her hands around the boy's head.

"Mom, no!" yelled the boy.

"Oh god!" yelled Angie, reaching for the boy. Freeda screamed and Angie turned back. The trucker's teeth had almost found skin.

Angie looked at the boy, then back at Freeda.

Back at the boy.

Then she ran to help Freeda. Her chest was tight as she grabbed the trucker's hand and bent his middle finger back. She pulled until the finger let out a harsh 'pop' and gave no more resistance. The trucker didn't respond.

Angie and Freeda struggled with the trucker. Somewhere behind them, the boy was shrieking. *Oh god, oh Jesus, I'm sorry*, Angie thought. She grabbed another of the trucker's fingers and broke it backward. The trucker's face showed no reaction, but his grip was now loose enough for Freeda to wriggle free.

"You okay?" said Angie, still holding the trucker's hand.

"Yep," said Freeda, putting a foot on the trucker's side and shoving. The trucker toppled over and Angie let go.

Angie turned. The boy was gone.

"The boy..." she started.

"We have to go," said Freeda, putting a hand on her shoulder from behind. The crazies approaching from the exit door were close now.

Angie swallowed, nodded, and turned to run back up the hall. Freeda followed.

Further up the hall, Park and Moe stood with a man who looked familiar. Park was yelling something. Angie blinked and recognized the man. Sam Shuab.

Angie and Freeda reached the arguing men.

"Listen, shithead," Park was saying. "I don't give a shit about you or how the fuck you're getting out of here. Now let me and my friend pass!"

Sam noticed Angie. "You! How the fuck do we get out of here?"

Park took advantage of Sam's distraction and pushed past him, pulling Moe with him.

"Sir," Angie started, "We gotta..."

"Thanks for all the help, kitten shit!" came Mr. Paulson's voice from Angie's side. She looked and saw him sitting in a wheelchair pushed by Kristen. Mr. Paulson's oxygen tank was strapped to the back of the wheelchair. Behind them, Mr. Paulson's room was in chaos. A crazy was stuck halfway in the window, impaled on a large piece of broken glass but still moving. Other crazies were trying to get in the window but were blocked by the impaled one.

Sam turned to Mr. Paulson. "For shit's sake, I'm trying to figure out the way out of here."

"Anj..." came Freeda's worried voice from behind Angie. The crazies behind them sounded very close.

"Follow me," said Angie, pushing past Sam. "I'll explain."

"Who the fuck died and left you in charge?" said Sam.

"Everyone."

She didn't look behind her, rushing to the nurse's station and assuming everyone was following her. She was right. She waited while everyone filed inside, then locked the door. She hoped no one could see her hands shaking.

She turned. Park was heading down the one remaining hall.

"That way," said Freeda, motioning the others down it.

"Freeda, wait..." Angie started.

"What the fuck!" came Park's voice from the hallway. The others disappeared down it.

Angie sighed and followed.

The others were standing, staring at the empty hall. And at the lack of a door at the end.

"There's no door!" yelled Park.

"This hall's on a hill," said Angie. "We only use it when the other rooms are full."

"The windows!" yelled Freeda, racing into one of the empty patient rooms.

"How the prick am I gonna get out a window?" yelled Mr. Paulson from his wheelchair.

Freeda came back out, shaking her head. "Those people. They're all along the walls down below. They just can't get to the windows."

Sam spun around, face deep red, and stomped to Angie. And balled up his large hand and punched her in the face.

"Bitch! You trapped us!"

"Hey!" yelled Park, letting go of Moe and running up. He punched Sam across the jaw. "The fuck's your problem?"

Sam stepped back, sputtering. "Fuck your mother's asshole, trailer trash. You know who I am?"

"I do," said Park, then punched him again. "That's for the shitty truck."

Angie's nose smarted. She felt blood coming. Freeda ran over to her.

"Shit, are you okay?"

Angie started to nod when Moe swayed and fell over backward.

"Moe!" yelled Park, rushing to him.

Muffled screams came from the nurse's station. Angie wiped her bloody nose and ran to see.

Behind the glass door, the little boy was lying on the floor.

"Shit!" said Angie, then went to unlock the door. She stopped, hand on the lock, when she saw the crazies behind the boy.

"Help!" the boy pleaded.

The boy's mother, eyes empty and cold, fell on the boy and bit into the back of his head. He shrieked and blood sprayed onto the glass.

"Oh god," came Freeda's voice behind her.

Angie slid to her knees. The boy grasped weakly at the glass. Angie put her hand to his, no longer caring if anyone saw her shake and cry.

Ten

For nearly half an hour, they all just sat and stared. Behind the three shut glass doors, people moaned and ran their hands along the glass. Angie moved her gaze from one door to another as she leaned against the nurse's desk.

"Call the cops again," said Sam.

"They're not answering," said Angie. "But surely they know. The whole hospital is under attack. Surely they know."

"What about your kids?" said Freeda beside her.

"No answer at home. They're probably out getting pizza or something. Brooke said they might. I just hope they don't see this on the news and freak out."

Kristen was leaning on the handles of Mr. Paulson's wheelchair. "I bet the cops are outside right now."

"They're dead," said Park, standing just inside the doorway leading to the empty hall. Moe was in the first patient room, resting. Freeda patted Angie on the shoulder, then walked down the hall to tend to Moe.

"How in the hell would you know whether the cops are dead?" said Sam.

"Not the cops," said Park. He took a step into the room and nodded at the glass doors. "Those fuckers. I think they're dead."

Mr. Paulson let out something between a laugh and a snort. "Listen, son. I know I may look dead, but I'm actually not. Know how you can tell, dumb shit? I'm fucking moving."

Sam chuckled.

"You can shut up too, shit bag," said Mr. Paulson. "You wouldn't know shit if it came out of your ass and slid down your leg."

Sam glared at Mr. Paulson. Kristen shook her head at Sam, then stroked her father's head.

"Now, Dad, don't get excited."

Park ignored all this and stepped closer to the doors. "Some of these fuckers are hurt. Too hurt to be walking."

Angie looked. Park had a point. A ridiculous point, but still a point.

"My god," said Kristen. Angie looked over to see her staring at the doors. Angie followed her gaze to a teenage girl standing outside one of the doors. The girl was wearing a torn and dirty dress and her lips looked glued together.

"I know her," said Kristen. "I mean, I knew of her. She was killed in a car accident. I saw the burial notice in the paper."

Angie saw Sam look and frown. He said nothing.

Park looked at Sam and Mr. Paulson. "You think she got better? Maybe she should have told the mortician before he glued her mouth shut."

"That must not be her," said Sam.

"It's her," said Kristen.

"For shit's sake," said Mr. Paulson. "If she's walking, she's not dead. I *can't* walk and *I'm* not fucking dead."

Park snorted and looked at Angie. "You got one of those stethoscope things?"

Angie opened a drawer in the nurse's desk. "There's one in here. Why?"

"Here's why," said Park. He walked to the glass door and pulled open the locks.

"Hey!" said Angie.

"Hold your shit, this'll be quick." Park pulled the door open, yanked the teen girl inside and shut the door before any of the others could get in.

"Catch," said Park, pushing the girl at Sam.

"What the hell is the matter with you!" yelled Angie.

Sam took a step back but caught the girl by the shoulders. "You crazy fuck!"

The girl moaned through her glued lips.

Park locked the door and turned.

The girl's lips separated, thick black blood and dried glue falling from her mouth. She groaned at Sam.

"Shit!" said Sam.

"Here," said Park. He grabbed the girl's shoulder from behind and kicked her legs. Sam let her go and the girl fell backward to the floor. Park held her down by her shoulders, kneeling behind her.

The girl hissed and bit at Park. "Shit," he said, avoiding her mouth and struggling to keep her down. "She's stronger than I would have thought."

"Get her the hell out of here!" said Angie.

"One second," said Park. He looked at Sam, who was staring down at him and the girl. "Hold her fucking legs, genius!"

Sam flashed red. "Fuck you, asshole."

"Unless you want her to get up and eat your fucking dad or whoever the fuck that is in the chair, hold her fucking legs."

"You're out of your goddamned mind," said Sam, getting down on his knees and taking hold of the girl's kicking legs.

Angie was stunned at the stupidity she was witnessing. "What the hell is the point of all this supposed to be?"

Park smirked at her. "Proving a point. Get the stethoscope."

Angie rolled her eyes. "Are you shitting me? That's what you risked opening the door for?"

"Just get it."

Angie sighed and took the stethoscope out of the nurse's desk. She walked over to where Park and Sam where holding the girl down.

Angie knelt and looked down at the girl. Seeing her up close made Angie feel cold. The girl's skin was gray and pasty. Her eyes were clouded and vacant. And she looked familiar.

From an obituary in the newspaper.

Angie put the stethoscope in her ears and leaned over the girl.

The girl hissed and snapped her teeth at Angie as she put the stethoscope to the girl's chest and listened.

She listened longer than she needed to.

Finally, she sighed and sat back, removing the stethoscope. "And?" said Park.

"No heartbeat," said Angie. "Nothing. And except for when she makes noise, it doesn't even sound like she's breathing."

"My god," said Kristen.

The room was quiet for a few moments, save the hissing and moaning of the girl.

"Ok," said Sam. "She's dead. Great. The whole world's gone fucking crazy and I'm holding a corpse down to keep it from eating me."

"Yep," said Park.

"Ok, genius," said Sam. "You let her in. She's dead. How in the holy fuck do we kill her again?"

"I know," said Angie. She stood and strode back to the nurse's station. She pulled the fire extinguisher from the wall and stepped back over. She slammed the extinguisher down on the girl's head.

"Jesus!" said Sam, letting go and sitting back.

The girl gurgled and moaned, moving more slowly now. Angie heaved the extinguisher back up and brought it down again. The girl's head collapsed, brain and black blood shooting out to one side.

"Jesus!" repeated Sam, jumping up and backing away.

The girl's hands fell to either side. She was still.

Park let go of the girl and raised his eyebrows. "How'd you know that?"

"Rick," said Angie, standing and dropping the extinguisher.

"What?"

"At the dispatch desk. His...head was crushed by the ambulance. He's the only one who didn't get back up."

Park nodded and stood. "Well, okay. Hopefully the cops bring lots of fire extinguishers."

Mr. Paulson snorted. "Those dick-sniffers. What passes for cops around here probably got eaten in the parking lot half an hour ago."

"They have guns," said Angie. "I bet just shooting the brain would kill these things."

"This is crazy," said Sam, pacing and continually glancing down at the dark slick of blood and brain on the floor. "In-fucking-sane. Where in the hell are they all even coming from?"

Park shrugged. "This one was buried, right? Isn't there a graveyard right by the hospital?"

Angie nodded.

Mr. Paulson laughed. "Sure as shit there is. Always thought the peckers here got a little something if they let patients die and gave the mortician some business."

Angie felt cold. "Oh shit."

"What?" said Park.

"There's graveyards all over this town."

Park shrugged again. "Lots of old people. Lots of dying."

"What if this is happening all over town?" said Angie, pulling out her cell phone. "Oh shit. I have to call home."

She dialed and waited.

Eleven

Maylee heard the phone ringing from the kitchen and did her best to ignore it.

"The phone's ringing," said Dalton. He was sitting on the toilet tank with his feet on the seat.

"Thanks for letting us know," said Maylee, sitting on the sink and twirling her bat one way and then the other. "Why don't you open the door and answer it?"

The phone rang a few more times then stopped. Moaning and scratching came from the door. Brooke was standing with her back to the door, rubbing her temples.

"Just keep quiet, you two," she said. "All we need to do is wait for the cops."

"The cops you can't call?" said Maylee.

Brooke flashed her a look. "They have to be coming. What's happening outside is too big. Someone had to have called. They're coming."

"Not necessarily," said Dalton, staring at the door. "What if this is happening all over town?"

A realization flashed through Maylee. "Oh shit," she said. She hopped off the sink to stand. "That's right! Mom could be in trouble. We have to get out of here."

Brooke sighed. "Maylee, please. You saw those people."

"I'll knock 'em in the head," said Maylee, brandishing her bat.

"There's too many," said Brooke.

"They aren't people, either," said Dalton.

"Don't say that," said Brooke. "They're people. There's just something wrong with them. They're sick or something."

"No," said Dalton. "This is worse than sick. That guy with no eyes?"

Maylee lowered the bat, thinking. "Yeah. And the arm that ripped off with no blood."

They all fell silent and listened to the groaning outside the door. Brooke looked like she was thinking. "That old lady. The one that attacked me outside. Her skin felt like a dead person's."

Dalton wrinkled his nose. "What are you doing touching dead people?"

"Shhh," said Maylee, her mind turning. "Wait...are you thinking those things are dead?"

Brooke shook her head. "No, that's crazy."

"It was crazy already," said Maylee. "Them being dead would just be more crazy to add to the crazy pile."

"Big pile," said Dalton.

"Huge," said Maylee.

"Will you two please keep quiet," said Brooke. "I'm trying to think."

Hell you are, thought Maylee. *You're just trying to look like you're thinking. We're on our own here.*

The phone rang again.

"Dammit," said Maylee. "That might be Mom. She might be in trouble."

"*We're* in trouble, Maylee!" snapped Brooke. "We're trapped in your bathroom with a crazed mob outside the door. Just back off for a second, ok?"

Maylee fumed but shrugged. She took a step back and leaned against the sink.

Brooke frowned and rubbed her arms. "And why the hell is it so cold in here?"

"Heat's broken in the bathroom," said Dalton, buttoning up his over-shirt.

"Mom's been on the landlord to fix it," said Maylee. "But he's a lazy dick."

"Wait..." said Dalton. He hopped off the toilet tank and walked to the bathtub. A large fuzzy mat was in front of it. Dalton knelt down and pulled the mat away, revealing a large rusted grate.

"What's that?" said Brooke.

"Heating grate," said Dalton.

"So what's your point?" said Brooke.

"I think I could squeeze through."

Maylee rolled her eyes. "And what, crawl around in the ducts? You're a little dork, but you're not that little."

"No," said Dalton. "The duct's loose, remember? That's what Mom's been on the landlord about."

Maylee thought about that.

"And the basement is unfinished," said Dalton. "I've been down there when Mom was complaining. The duct is just barely hanging on."

Maylee frowned. Brooke shook her head.

"Dammit," said Dalton. "Look."

Dalton tugged at the grate. It was loose but didn't come free.

"Give me a toothbrush or something," he said.

"You ain't touching my toothbrush."

"Then give me mine, geez!"

Maylee shrugged and pulled Dalton's toothbrush from a cup next to the faucet. She handed it to him.

Dalton wedged the toothbrush in one of the slots on the grate. He pulled on it, then again. On the third time the grate popped free.

Brooke raised her eyebrows.

"See," said Maylee to her. "Lazy dick."

"Now, watch," said Dalton. He put one leg into the hole and slammed his foot down. The ductwork creaked and groaned.

He grinned and did it again. A louder, longer creak came.

"Crap," he said, then slammed his foot down a third time. His leg slipped further down the hole and a loud clatter came from below the bathroom.

"Shit," said Brooke, rushing over and pulling Dalton up by the shoulders. "Are you okay?"

"I'm fine," said Dalton, wriggling away.

Brooke knelt and looked down the hole. "What's down there?"

"The basement," said Maylee, leaning over next to her. "And he's right. If he just kicked the duct off, that hole goes straight down to it."

"Right," said Brooke. "I'll go down."

"What?" laughed Dalton. "You can't fit."

"I'm the adult," said Brooke. "I'll take the risk."

"You're not an adult," said Maylee.

"I'm the closest thing we've got!" yelled Brooke.

"You won't fit!" yelled Dalton.

"Neither will you," said Maylee. "I'm skinnier than you are."

"You have boobs."

Maylee flashed red. "You little freakin' perv!"

They all stopped yelling. The groans from outside the door had been steadily getting louder.

Brooke listened, then looked at Dalton and Maylee. "We have to be quiet. They can hear us in here and there's no reason to make them any crazier."

"You...won't...fit," whispered Dalton.

Brooke looked at the hole, then at Dalton, then at Maylee. Then back at Dalton. "Shit. This is insane. If you got down there, could you get outside?"

Dalton nodded. "The door locks from the inside. I can get out and into the backyard."

Brooke sighed. "Fine. You get as far away as you can and get an adult."

"No," whispered Dalton, looking shocked. "I'm getting the phone so we can call Mom."

The phone rang again. Maylee sighed and leaned toward Brooke. "We can distract those things. Make noise so he can get the phone then get back to the basement."

Brooke looked at Maylee and swallowed. *She's scared,* Maylee realized.

The phone stopped ringing.

Twelve

Angie snapped her phone shut. She felt like crying.

Freeda put a hand on her shoulder. "I'm sure they're fine."

They were both sitting on the nurse's desk, facing the doors. Corpses groaned and clawed at each of the three glass planes.

"Dead, huh?" said Freeda, staring at them.

"Yeah," said Angie.

"So Jimmy was dead the whole time?"

Angie nodded and bit her thumb.

"Damn."

Angie dropped her hand. "Yeah."

"Dammit," said Park, walking in from the empty hallway. "Moe looks awful. We have to get out of here."

Mr. Paulson chuckled from his wheelchair. "And take him where, numbnuts, the hospital?"

"We know how to kill them," said Park, nodding at the corpses clawing at the glass. "Why can't we just make a run for it?"

Kristen shook her head and adjusted the oxygen tube on Mr. Paulson's face. "We couldn't move Dad that quickly."

"Or your friend," said Freeda.

"Then we need guns," said Park.

"Yeah," said Mr. Paulson. "A wrecking ball and a fucking helicopter would be nice too."

"Now, Dad," said Kristen. "They're just trying to help." She stroked his head.

"Get your fucking over-lotioned hands off of me," Mr. Paulson grumbled, twisting his head away. "Point is, we don't have any guns."

"I've got guns in my truck," said Park.

Sam, who'd been sulking against a wall, stepped toward Park. "Great. The truck in the parking lot? If we could get to the parking lot, we wouldn't be having this conversation."

"No," said Park. "We all couldn't make it, but one or two of us might. Get some guns back here, then we can use them to clear a path for the others."

Sam shook his head. "This is crazy."

"Yeah," said Angie, "but it's better than nothing."

"How would we even get to the parking lot?" said Sam. "The hallways are full of those things."

"Watch," said Park. He fished his lighter out of his pocket and stepped over to the door. He flicked it on and held the flame to the glass. The corpses on the other side backed away from the flame. "Noticed this in the parking lot. These things don't like fire."

Sam looked at the lighter, then at Angie. "You said you think we just have to damage the brain, right? I bet fire would kill these fuckers, too. Cook their brains."

Park nodded. "Maybe we can rig up some torches or something to hold them back."

Angie pushed herself off the desk and walked over. "You'd just set off the sprinklers and end up wet and eaten. And besides, there's another way out."

She walked over to a utility closet and opened it. Inside were a mop bucket, some gloves and a chain to turn the light on. She grabbed the chain and pulled. Park walked up behind her.

"Ok," said Angie. She looked up and found a leather strap hanging from the ceiling of the closet. She pulled and a wooden ladder unfolded downward. She stepped back to let it connect to the floor.

"And where's that go?" said Park.

"The roof," said Angie. "To allow work crews quick access to the lights up there. And not only that. There's another, metal ladder attached to the side of the building for the same purpose. And it goes right down to the parking lot."

"Well fuck-a-doo," said Park, looking at the ladder and nodding. He stepped back into the room. "Okay. Looks like we're taking the roof."

Angie walked over to Park. "I'll come with you."

Sam laughed. "No offense, but you'll need someone tougher than..."

"Hey, funny story," said Park. "Remember about fifteen minutes ago when she pounded one's head in while you shit your pants?"

Mr. Paulson laughed. "I love that story."

Sam went red. "Listen, I don't trust this prick to come back even if he does get to his damn truck."

"We don't have time for this," said Angie. "I have no idea if my kids are in trouble or not. We have to get out of here!"

Sam turned on her. "And what's stopping you from bolting home the second you get outside?"

Park made a growling noise. "Listen, dickburger, my friend's in that room back there..."

"Well, my wife's here!" said Sam. "So I guess we'll both be coming back."

Angie opened her mouth, then looked at Freeda. Freeda was looking at the floor, her hands clenched together.

She stepped over to Freeda. "You ok?"

"Yeah," said Freeda, looking up at her. "Just make sure you get back quick."

Angie looked at Freeda, then over at Park and Sam.

"Hey," she said. "Let Sam go with you. I'll stay. Your friend will need Freeda and me to look after him. Maybe the two of us will add up to a real nurse."

Sam shot her a look.

"Whatever," said Park. "Let me go check in with Moe, then me and dick-face'll make a run for it."

Thirteen

"Are you sure about this?" said Maylee, peering through the hole in the floor. "I can't see jack or squat down there."

"I'll be fine," said Dalton, standing impatiently next to her. "I'll be able to find my way to the door."

"And then you run to a neighbor's," said Brooke, next to the

razy?" said Dalton, looking at Brooke. "You saw it
ighbor's won't be any safer."
't like this," Brooke said.
," said Maylee. "But he's the only one who would

's an old ladder down there," said Dalton. "I'll get
back up here, then we can call Mom."
ops," said Brooke.
army," said Maylee.
hed. "Okay. We'll bang on the door and keep them
ou get into the kitchen, get the phone, then get back

dded and smiled.
ou so happy about?" said Maylee.
are doing my idea."

"Whoopie-doo," said Maylee, smirking. "Get in the hole."

Dalton stepped over to the hole grinning.

A woman outside the door groaned, loud and gurgling on some kind of fluid. Blood, Maylee figured. Maybe bile. It sent a cold spasm up Maylee's back.

Both she and Dalton stopped smiling.

"Let's go," said Brooke. "And please, be careful."

Dalton sat next to the hole and put both legs down it.

The scratching outside the door grew louder. Maylee looked at the door and frowned. "Are there more of them now?"

"God, I hope not," said Brooke.

Dalton put his palms on the floor and eased himself down into the hole. He got to just above his waist and stopped.

"Uh-oh," he said.

"Uh-oh what?" said Maylee.

"I can't get past here," said Dalton.

"What?" said Maylee.

"Oh crap," said Dalton. "I can't go up, either. I'm stuck."

The groaning from outside grew louder.

"Ok, wait," said Brooke, stepping up. "Don't panic."

"Crap," said Dalton, looking around. "Where's the groaning coming from?"

"Outside," said Maylee, grabbing hold of Dalton's arm. "Same as before."

"You sure it's not from under me?" said Dalton, real panic creeping into his eyes. "Oh god, I gotta get out of here."

Loud moans came from behind the door.

"I can hear them down there!" yelled Dalton, struggling.

"They're outside," said Brooke. "Just hang on."

Maylee pulled. Dalton wouldn't budge.

"Ow!" yelled Dalton.

"Shit!" yelled Maylee, letting go. "What happened?"

"You hurt my arm," said Dalton, rubbing it.

Maylee sighed. "Damn it, I thought something bit you, you little shit!" She balled up a fist and bopped Dalton on the top of the head.

There was a "pop" and Dalton slid further down the hole.

All three of them screamed.

"What the hell happened?" yelled Dalton.

Maylee noticed a small shirt button at the corner of the room and let out a sigh. "It's okay. It was just a button coming off your shirt."

"Oh," said Dalton, "Okay. Then..."

And with a fast series of "pops" Dalton slid the rest of the way down the hole. Dalton's chin smacked the side of the hole on the way down.

"Dalton!" yelled Maylee as he vanished from view. A crumpled "whump" came from under the room.

Maylee dropped to her knees and looked through the hole. In the small rectangle of light the hole provided, she could see Dalton's head. He was on his back, facing the ceiling. His eyes were shut.

"Dalton!" yelled Maylee.

Dalton didn't move.

Groaning and scratching came from outside the door.

Fourteen

Park pushed open the door to the roof and cursed under his breath. Moe had looked bad. Real bad. He paused on the ladder, smelling the night air and listening. He heard groaning and smelled rot, but nothing that seemed close by. That was good. If the corpses could climb up onto roofs, Park and the others would be extra fucked.

"See anything?" said Sam from behind him on the ladder.

"The sky," said Park, then climbed the rest of the way up onto the roof.

Up here, Park could smell the rotting corpses and hear their groaning even more. It sounded like the fuckers were everywhere.

He stepped away from the opening and Sam climbed up after him.

"Damn," he said, rubbing his arms in the cold air. "Fucking stinks up here."

"Aren't you just full of useful information?" said Park. He turned around, scanning all corners of the roof, trying to get his bearings. Finally he stopped and pointed. "The most light seems to be coming from that way, so I'm betting that's the parking lot."

Park strode that direction, not bothering to check if Sam was following him.

Damn it, Moe had looked bad.

They reached the edge of the roof and looked down. It was indeed the parking lot. A few corpses were wandering around, but it looked like most of them had already crowded their way into the hospital.

"Damn," said Sam as he looked down. "Seems high from up here. Doesn't this place only have the one floor?"

"Yeah," said Park. "There's probably ductwork and crap between the ceiling and the roof, too, though. Adds several feet. Plus, you're a pussy."

"Fuck you."

Park looked to his left and saw the rounded top of a metal ladder bolted into the roof. "That would be the ladder," he said.

He went to the ladder and looked over the side. The ladder ran straight down to the pavement of the parking lot. He looked around and saw his truck, parked over by the emergency room. Even with the ladder depositing them right onto the parking lot, it would still be quite a run. The few corpses wandering around would have plenty of time to notice and come after them.

Moe had barely been able to talk. His voice had sounded like he was choking.

"Okay," said Park, pointing. "There's the truck. We'll have to move fast."

"Fuck," said Sam, looking from the bottom of the ladder to the truck. "You would have to park so far away."

"Yeah, I should have considered having to climb down from the roof to avoid walking corpses. Now shut the fuck up and let's go."

Park climbed onto the ladder first, swinging around to face Sam and putting his feet on the topmost rung.

"Okay," he started, then stopped when the lights on the roof and in the parking lot flickered.

"Shit," said Sam, looking around. "Be all we'd need to have the fucking power go out."

Park grunted and nodded.

And down they went. Slowly, hand over hand, Park descended the ladder. Sam was several rungs above him. Park could smell rotting flesh and blood, but the moans were still relatively far away. So far, so good. As long as the light held...

And then the lights went out. All around Park went black. Seriously black. No nearby lights worked and the sky was overcast, obscuring moon and stars.

"Shit!" said Sam from above. "Can't see a fucking thing!"

"Damn it!" Park said, stopping his climbing. "Just stop up there. Hopefully it'll come back."

"How far did we get?"

"Not sure. Close, I think."

"Shit. Maybe we should jump for it."

Park's hands were slippery with sweat. "Don't be a fucking idiot. If you sprain your ankle or some shit, I ain't stopping for you."

"Let's go back up."

"Dammit, just stay where you are... wait, do you smell that?"

"What?" said Sam. "Just the same stink of those rotting fuckers."

"Yeah, but it's stronger..."

The lights flickered back on just as Park was looking down. A corpse closed its hand on Park's foot and pulled him off the ladder.

Park hit the pavement stomach first. It hurt and the air rushed from his lungs, but there was no time to worry about it. The corpse was behind him, moaning and squeezing his leg. Soon it would be biting.

Park rolled over as best he could and kicked at the corpse. It was a man, bloated and slimy. He wore a blue button-up shirt that was torn and rotted. Fresh dirt clung to his body and clothes in thick clumps. *This one's been buried a while*, Park thought.

He took a quick glance up and saw Sam still clinging to the ladder, looking down with wide eyes. *Useless*. Park kicked at the bloated man with his free leg. The bloated man's head whipped back with a cracking noise and he let go. Park pulled his leg away and stood. The bloated man squirmed on the pavement, his head lolling around loosely. Park kicked again, hard. The man's skull caved on one side and he was still.

Sam was climbing down the ladder behind him. "Thanks for all the help," said Park, turning to look at him.

Sam blinked and turned red. "You know damned good and well that happened too fast to do anything..."

"Whatever," said Park. "Just don't shoot yourself from shaking so bad when you get a gun."

Park turned and headed for his truck. Why was he even bothering? He'd been planning on killing himself earlier today, why hadn't he just let the bloated thing do it?

Damn it, Moe had looked bad.

"You know what?" said Sam from behind him. "I'm getting really sick of your bullshit."

Park stopped and turned. Sam stopped and looked at him. "You really want to do this now?" said Park. "You want to have this discussion right fucking now?"

And a corpse came out from behind a car and grabbed Sam from behind. It was a young girl in a cheerleader outfit. One of the two Park had seen earlier.

"Shit!" yelled Sam. The cheerleader moved her mouth to Sam's neck. Park stepped over and punched the girl in the forehead. She stopped, blinked and hissed at him

Sam pulled away and stepped back. "Damn it! I can't take this disgusting shit."

"Goddammit, get something heavy!" yelled Park.

Sam glared at him, then rushed off. From the corner of his eye, Park could see Sam rooting around in the back of a nearby pickup. Park watched the girl. She moaned and reached for him, but slowly enough that Park could keep clear of her. Finally, Sam rushed back over with a crowbar.

"Here," Sam said, handing it to Park.

Park glanced over at Sam. "Really? You're giving it to me? She's right there. You could do it."

"I can't handle this disgusting shit!"

"You gotta be fucking kidding me," said Park. He took the crowbar and slammed it down on the cheerleader's head. She shook from the force. Her arms twitched. Then she collapsed to the ground, still.

"Go team," said Park.

He turned to look at Sam. The big man was adjusting his glasses and staring at the collapsed cheerleader. "Here," said Park, handing him the crowbar. "This is for cheerleaders. Now let's go."

They walked the rest of the way to Park's truck in silence. It sat where Park had left it, crooked in a handicapped spot in front of the emergency room doors.

"Nice parking," said Sam from behind him. Park fished out his keys and unlocked the door. The door creaked as he pulled it open. Park reached inside and found the two hunting rifles he and Moe had been using.

Moe had barely been able to speak when Park had last seen him, lying on the hospital bed in that empty room.

Moe's lips had been dry and his voice hoarse. "I'm not going to make it, Park."

"Sure you will," Park had said, knowing full well it was bullshit but not knowing what else to say. Not knowing what else to think.

"You know better than that," Moe had said. "Listen, Park. If you get a chance to get out of here, take it. Don't die because of me. Just go."

In the parking lot, Park turned and handed Sam a gun. "Here. You can use this on cheerleaders too." He set the other gun down in the passenger seat, then leaned over to open the glove compartment. He pulled out a box of ammo and straightened back up.

He turned and handed the box to Sam. Sam slung the rifle over one shoulder and took the box.

"You might want to put the ammo in your pocket," said Park.

"Why?"

"So you don't drop it."

"Why would I drop it?

"Because I'm about to punch you in the face." And Park did. As hard as he could.

Sam staggered back, surprised. Park took the moment to climb into the truck and shut the door. *Just go*.

"What the fuck?" Sam sputtered from outside.

"Best of luck," said Park, starting the engine. He'd take a short drive home, then off himself on his own terms. He was done. He'd been done all day, he'd just been delayed.

Park put the truck in reverse and backed out of the spot. *Surprised I didn't get a ticket*, he thought, smirking to himself. He pulled away, driving for the road.

In the rearview mirror, Sam was screaming something at him. Park watched Sam's face turn red. Finally Sam gave up and ran back for the ladder.

"Best of luck," Park repeated to the empty truck.

Park reached the road and stopped out of habit, looking for oncoming traffic before he turned. He looked in the rearview mirror and saw Sam reach the ladder. He was climbing. Two corpses had followed him and were grabbing at his legs. A third was approaching. Sam was struggling.

Park sighed at the mirror. "Dumb ass." Then he looked at the road again. It was clear. He could turn.

But he didn't. He looked at the mirror instead. The corpses were still grabbing at Sam. Sam was still on the ladder but probably wouldn't be for long.

Park looked back at the road.

Then at the mirror.

"Shit goddammit hell," said Park, and threw the truck in reverse.

He spun around in the parking lot and sped for the ladder. The truck groaned and clattered as it hit bumps and potholes, but Park didn't slow down. Sam saw the truck coming and started climbing as fast as he could. Park chuckled, sounding and feeling a little crazy. Not really knowing why, he reached down and fastened his seat belt.

"Gotta buckle up," he said to himself.

Then he slammed the truck into the bottom of the ladder. The corpses went splat underneath him. One flew off to one side, groaning as its legs came free from its torso.

The seat belt dug into Park's shoulder as the force of the crash flung him forward. The engine sputtered and hissed. Park eased himself back and shut off the ignition.

"You goddamn crazy fucking trailer trash idiot!" came Sam's screams from above him, up on the ladder. "What in the holy name of fuck is wrong with you?"

"Just saving your ass," said Park, unhooking the seat belt and reaching for the rifle next to him. "Fuck knows why, but that's what I'm doing."

Corpses were already closing in on the truck. *They must be coming from inside,* Park thought. *All this noise must be bringing them out.*

The ladder creaked above him. "Dammit!" yelled Sam. "You knocked the ladder loose!"

Park looked out the windows to each side. Two or three corpses were clawing at the glass. *I could shoot them,* he thought as he opened the glove compartment and pulled out a second box of ammo. He stuck the ammo in his pocket. *But no point in wasting ammo.*

He slid down in the seat and kicked at the windshield. With a few kicks the glass splintered and came free.

The ladder creaked again. "Shit!" said Sam.

"Just hurry and get up the fucking thing!" yelled Park. He climbed out the window and onto the hood. Corpses reached for him but the hood was too wide.

"Where the fuck were you going?" yelled Sam above him, climbing.

"A party," said Park. "With ice cream and a fucking clown. Just get the fuck up there!" He walked across the hood to the ladder and took hold. It gave a little too much. It *was* loose.

He looked up. Sam was halfway back to the roof. Park slung the rifle over his shoulder and started climbing.

From below him, Park heard his engine hiss and sputter, even though he'd turned it off. He doubted it'd be running again any time soon. Corpses groaned down there, too. Park didn't look.

The ladder swayed as he climbed. He got several rungs up before realizing Sam had stopped.

"What the hell are you doing?" said Park.

"We're gonna have to slow down," said Sam. "This thing's gonna give any second."

"Fuck it is. Fucker's made of steel or some shit. Just go!"

Sam grumbled and resumed climbing.

Park swore under his breath and followed.

The ladder gave a loud groan and separated from the roof.

"Shit!" yelled Sam as the ladder leaned backward. The corpses down below moaned as if waiting for the meals to drop.

Park swung around on the ladder, grabbing hold of the back. He leaned back toward the building as hard as he could. The ladder stopped, suspending them both in midair. "Do what I'm doing, dickless!" he yelled.

Sam did, climbing to the back of the ladder and leaning toward the wall. The ladder creaked and fell back the other way. Park's back slammed into the hospital wall.

"Ow!" yelled Sam.

The corpses below moaned.

"Now go!" said Park. "I'll hold it!"

Sam squirmed out from behind the ladder and climbed back onto the front. He climbed up as fast as he could until he reached the roof. Park saw him jump onto the roof, then turn to grab hold of the ladder's rounded top.

"Come on!" yelled Sam.

"I'm touched, Shuab," said Park to himself as he spun to the other side of the ladder and climbed. He made it to the top and hopped off next to Sam.

Sam let go and the ladder fell away from the building. With a loud creaking groan, the ladder dropped onto Park's truck. "Damn it, you broke the fucking ladder."

"Don't need the ladder anymore," said Park, smirking. "We have these." He patted the rifle on his shoulder.

Fifteen

"Dalton!" came Maylee's voice from the darkness.

No wait, not darkness, Dalton realized. His eyes were just shut. And his chin *really* hurt.

He opened his eyes. He was on his back in the basement, looking up at the hole he had made. He blinked at the blurry light from the hole. A shape was looking down at him. He blinked again and saw it was Maylee. He groaned and sat up.

"Shit," said Maylee. "Are you okay?"

"What happened?" he asked.

"You fell. And you've been like that for like ten minutes. I thought you were dead."

Brooke's head appeared next to the hole. "Is he awake?"

Dalton nodded up at them.

Brooke sighed. "Thank god. Now get back up here before you get really hurt. This was a terrible idea."

Dalton shook his head and climbed to his feet. "No way. This is working."

"Maybe she's right," said Maylee.

"No!" said Dalton, glaring up at her. "Let me do this! I can do this. And we'll get to talk to Mom because I did it."

He stepped away from the light of the hole, looking for another light. The unfinished basement was cluttered and dusty, with abandoned tools lying on the floor where the landlord had left them. Dalton knelt and found a wrench, then a rusty hammer, then a flashlight.

He clicked the flashlight on and a dim, dingy light came from it. Like the battery was weak. *Have to hurry*, he thought. *Battery won't last long.*

"Dalton!" came Maylee's voice.

Dalton stepped back into the light. "I found a flashlight!"

"Great," said Maylee. "You can use it to blind the dead people. Just get up here."

"Dammit, Maylee. Let me do this."

Maylee frowned down at him. Brooke appeared back in the hole. Maylee pushed her away. "Okay. Go. But be careful."

Dalton nodded, clicked on the flashlight, and stepped away from the light. He decided to check outside first.

Using the dim light in his hand, he slowly made his way to the door. The door had a small window with a curtain. He pulled the curtain back and peeked out. He couldn't see anything, so he stepped back and looked at the door itself. It was locked, just like he'd expected. He put an ear to the door and listened. Nothing. Or at least, nothing loud.

Then again, he realized, how loud would dead people be?

He grabbed the deadbolt and turned. The lock clicked open. Dalton stopped to listen. Again, nothing.

He drew in a breath and pushed the door slowly open.

The grass of his backyard greeted him. Dark and silent. The moonlight he'd seen before was gone. *Cloudy,* Dalton thought. *Just great.*

He stuck his head out to look around. Just in time to see a corpse stumble around the corner.

Crap! He snapped off the flashlight and ducked back inside, shutting the door as silently as he could. He heard the thing drawing near. He'd gotten a good look at it. It was the man they'd seen out the window earlier. The one with his head bent all the way back. So maybe it hadn't seen Dalton. Had it?

The shape of the corpse appeared in the door's window. It moaned, muffled by the wood of the door. It stopped just outside the window.

Crap. It saw me. Or it can smell me.

And he hadn't gotten a ladder ready to climb back up the hole. Was there even a ladder down here? How could he be so stupid?

He swallowed, his heart pounding, and stared at the shape in the window.

With a groan, the shape shuffled out of view.

Dalton breathed out. It hadn't noticed him.

He clicked the flashlight back on and scanned the basement for a ladder. He found one, rusting in a corner. He grabbed it and dragged it to the hole. It was the kind that opened to stand on its own, which was a relief. He opened it and placed it under the hole. He looked up at Maylee.

"Okay. All clear," he said. "You guys start banging in about five minutes."

Maylee nodded and disappeared from view.

Dalton drew himself up and turned to head for the door.

Sixteen

Angie heard movement coming from the utility closet. She stepped away from the nurse's desk and ran over.

Park was coming down the ladder, a rifle slung over one shoulder.

"My god," she said. "I can't believe that honestly worked."

Park snorted. "Thanks a lot." He stepped away from the ladder.

Kristen was kneeling by Mr. Paulson's wheelchair, helping Freeda check the oxygen tank. She stood up and walked over to the closet. "Sam? Where's Sam? We heard a lot of noise."

Sam appeared on the ladder. "I bet you did. That was genius-boy smashing the outside ladder. We aren't getting out that way now." He dropped to the bottom of the closet and adjusted his glasses.

"We weren't getting out that way before, anyway," said Park. He pulled a box of ammo from his pocket and started loading the rifle.

"Well, it's nice to have options," said Sam. He nodded to Kristen, who smiled and walked back over to Mr. Paulson.

"Okay," said Angie, checking her cell phone for any missed calls. There were none. "Let's get ready to move." She nodded to Freeda, who nodded back. *Dear God, let my kids be okay.*

Sam was frowning about something. "Give me a second," he said, stepping into the hallway. "Gotta get this thing loaded."

* * *

Sam stepped into the hallway and fumbled with his gun. Dammit, Kristen hadn't even touched him. He'd nearly died out there, and she hadn't even touched him.

Her dad. Always her dad. She barely looked at Sam anymore.

Of course he'd said okay when the old man needed to move in. How could he not? But the old man took so much damned time and attention. Sam was forty-five and childless. They'd never have children at this rate. Hell, the old man *was* their child. A vulgar, hateful child.

Hot tears stung his eyes and he took off his glasses to rub them. No time for this. No time for crying or for being a whiny little bitch about life. Time to man up.

He put the glasses back on and felt around in his pocket for the box of ammo.

Moaning came from the nearest patient room.

Panic shot up Sam's back. How'd those things get inside? How many of them were there?

Then he realized. It was just Park's friend.

He breathed out and started to the others for help. Then he cursed himself.

Fuck, does the pussy need help checking on some sick asshole? Dammit, Shuab, be a man!

He sighed and stepped into the patient room.

The sick guy was lying on the bed, moving his head from side to side. The guy's eyes were cloudy and his mouth chewed slowly at nothing.

"Hey, Moe? It is Moe, right? Are you okay?"

Moe said nothing. He moved his head around and moaned. He hadn't blinked since Sam had entered.

"Looks like we'll be getting out of here soon, thanks to your buddy's guns," Sam continued.

Moe said nothing.

"Well, fuck you then. What do I look like, a nurse?"

Sam turned to leave. Moe let out a long groan.

Sam turned back. "Shit, that sounded bad. You okay?" He stepped over to look down at Moe.

His glasses slipped down his nose. Sam cursed and took them off. "Hate these things."

Moe sat up and bit.

Moe's teeth closed on Sam's cheek and eye. Skin gave way and peeled back. Sam's eye was punctured. Blood and something thicker ran down Sam's cheek as his body shook involuntarily. Hot pain shot through Sam's head and for a moment he was too shocked to scream. Moe's head slid down to Sam's throat and bit. Sam felt a chunk of his neck pull free. He tried to scream then and couldn't. His voice box was gone. Moe moaned and chewed.

Sam's knees buckled and he dropped. Blood flowed fast. He tried crawling for the door. He was getting weak fast. Moe dropped off the bed onto Sam's back. Sam felt Moe biting into the back of his head. Scalp and hair tore away.

Oh shit, Kristen. Kristen. I'm sorry.

He felt dizzy. Far away from the sounds of Moe chewing. Then he was dead.

* * *

Angie spun away from Freeda as a loud "thump" came from the hallway. Everyone stopped what they were doing.

"Shit," she said. "What was that?"

"Dunno," said Park as he finished loading the rifle. He slung the gun over his shoulder. "Let's see."

Angie and Park rushed into the hallway, then turned to enter Moe's room. Angie gasped when she saw.

Moe straddled Sam's body, chewing at an open wound in the back of Sam's head. Sam's head rocked from side to side in rhythm with Moe's bites.

"Oh god," said Angie.

"Oh dammit, Moe," said Park.

Mr. Paulson's voice came from the nurse's station. "What the fuck is it now?"

Park took the rifle from his shoulder. Moe looked up at Park. He moaned, a hunk of Sam's flesh falling from his mouth.

Angie turned to Park. "Listen to me, Parker. He's not your friend anymore and..."

Park fired right through Moe's brain. Moe fell backward, legs splayed, and slumped against the side of the bed. His head fell to one side. He was still.

"Yeah," said Park, lowering the rifle. "No shit." Park sniffed and rubbed his eyes.

"Sam!" shrieked Kristen from behind them. She pushed past and rushed to Sam's body. "Oh god, god no! No!" She knelt and cradled his head. Blood and muck ran down her lap. "Honey! No!"

Angie swallowed. "I'm so sorry..."

"The hell you are!" Kristen yelled. "Sam was right! This *is* all your fault! You led us back here!"

"Listen lady," said Park, leveling the rifle at Sam. "You're going to have to move."

Kristen gasped and pulled Sam's body closer. "You keep away from him!"

"What the hell are you doing in there?" yelled Mr. Paulson from the nurse's station.

Freeda ran back and saw. "Oh shit."

Park sighed and lowered the gun. "What the fuck lady? He's already dead."

Kristen sobbed and clutched Sam's body. "You are NOT going to shoot him!"

Angie turned to Park. "Listen. It looks like the head's already injured, so maybe..."

Park shook his head. "Not deep enough. We have to be sure."

Angie turned back. Kristen was sobbing and rocking Sam's body back and forth. "Listen, Kristen..."

"Shut up!" Kristen shrieked.

"I'm all alone out here, dammit!" yelled Mr. Paulson from the nurse's station.

Kristen sobbed.

Angie spoke as softly as she could. "Kristen, we have to be sure. You saw what happened to Moe. If we aren't sure, he'll get back up and he won't be your husband." She felt like a fraud. If her kids were dead, she'd be done. Would she listen to anyone trying to give her perspective?

Please God, please, don't let my kids be dead.

Kristen looked down and sobbed.

"Will some-fucking-one please come help the crippled fucking old man!" yelled Mr. Paulson.

Kristen took a deep, ragged breath and nodded. "Okay. But let me do it."

Park frowned, lowering the rifle further. "You know how to use this?"

Kristen nodded and wiped her eyes. "I know enough."

Angie nodded and took the gun from Park. "Okay then. Here." She handed the rifle to Kristen. Kristen's hands shook as she took it.

"Thank you," said Kristen.

"We'll give you a moment," said Angie, turning back toward the door. Park was blocking the way.

He frowned at her. "You sure about this?"

Angie nodded. "Yeah. Let's go."

Angie, Park and Freeda moved slowly back out to the nurse's station. Mr. Paulson was complaining and yelling for his daughter, but Angie couldn't focus on the words. They all waited nearly ten minutes.

A shot came from the other room. And the sound of Kristen sobbing.

Seventeen

Dalton gripped the flashlight and opened the door. He saw only the backyard, silent and still. A little brighter now. *The moon must be back.* He snapped the flashlight off and stuck his head outside the door. He looked both ways. Nothing.

He took a deep breath. He heard Maylee and Brooke start banging on the bathroom door. He heard the corpses moan in response.

"Hey!" came Maylee's voice, sounding far away and muffled. "We're in here! Come and get us!"

Dalton ducked out the door and into the yard.

He took a moment to let his eyes adjust to the moonlight and to listen. He heard moaning here and there, but nothing close. He swallowed and headed for the side of the house.

Rounding the corner, he saw nothing. He sighed in relief and walked as quietly as he could up the side of the house. He stopped at the corner, where he could see the street.

A few corpses were wandering up the street. At least Dalton assumed they were corpses. They moved too slowly and too strangely to be human. None of them saw Dalton.

He heard screams somewhere far off. Voices he didn't recognize. Screams of pain or fear. Maybe an alarm, too far away to be sure.

He steeled up his courage and poked his head around the corner. The front yard looked clear. He smiled and stepped out, facing the side of the front stoop.

Cold hands closed on his throat from behind.

Without thinking, Dalton dropped to his knees. The move was out of panic more than anything else, but he slipped free of the corpse's fingers. He spun onto his rear and looked up.

It was a woman with blond hair and ...

Dalton blinked.

Mrs. Harris. His teacher. He recognized her blond hair and green eyes, but the bottom half of her face was torn to shreds. A wet cavity of blood and meat. Her tongue flopped from side to side. Two bones on each side of her face, what was left of her jaw, worked up and down. She reached for him.

Dalton screamed, clambered to his feet, and ran.

He ran to the front porch and looked inside. The living room was a wreck. A big group of corpses was clustered outside the bathroom door, groaning at Maylee and Brooke as they banged on the door from inside. The corpses didn't notice him, but they were blocking the way to the kitchen. He'd have to use the side door, the one the eyeless man had come through.

He swallowed and hoped there weren't any corpses in there. Mrs. Harris gurgled at him from his right, reminding him to hurry.

He ran for the other side of the house. Fear of Mrs. Harris pushed him around the corner without stopping to look. He stopped when he realized what he was doing. It was clear. No corpses between him and the kitchen door. It swung to and fro, just as the corpses had apparently left it. He glanced back at Mrs. Harris. She was just past the front porch now, moving slowly and making a low choking growl.

Dalton sucked in his breath and ran for the kitchen. He stopped when he reached the door.

Through the doorway to the kitchen, Dalton could see the corpses crowding the bathroom. They were all in the hallway and the kitchen looked clear. He could see the phone in its cradle next to the microwave. The phone Brooke had used to call for the pizza.

As quietly as he could, he crept into the kitchen and headed for the phone.

He could hear Maylee and Brooke banging on the door. The corpses were focused on them. None of them noticed Dalton creeping up from behind. He was almost to the phone.

Groaning came from behind him. Dalton turned. The corpse from earlier, the one with his head bent all the way back, was standing in the doorway. The corpse's back faced Dalton, which meant the corpse's head faced Dalton. The corpse saw. He groaned at him.

Dalton screamed. The corpses in the hallway heard and turned and groaned at him. Corpses closed in on him from both sides.

* * *

Maylee was in the middle of hitting the door, hand raised in mid-strike, when Dalton's scream echoed through the house. The sound sent cold panic through her. She heard the corpses at the door change their focus, heard their groans now being directed at the kitchen. "Dalton!" she yelled.

"There's too many!" he yelled.

"I'm coming!" she yelled. She unlocked the door.

"Maylee, don't!" yelled Brooke, pulling Maylee back. "Let me do it! It's too dangerous."

Brooke opened the door. Over Brooke's shoulder, Maylee could see the corpses moving to the kitchen.

"Hey!" yelled Brooke. She kicked one of the corpses in the back. "Look, dumb-asses! More meat over here!"

The corpses turned to Brooke. Maylee could see Dalton in the kitchen, running away from the corpse with his head bent all the way back.

"That's right!" yelled Brooke at the corpses. "Come on!" She ran down the hallway. The corpses slowly followed her. Maylee stood as far back and as still as she could, amazed that none of them noticed her.

When the hallway was clear, Maylee snatched up her bat from the back of the toilet and ran for the kitchen. Dalton was barely avoiding the broken-neck corpse, which was stumbling around and grabbing at him.

Maylee ran up to the corpse and, screaming, slammed the thing across the head with her bat. The thing's head snapped up the other way, landing against the thing's chest. The corpse groaned, muffled now, and stumbled away. She ran to Dalton and grabbed him.

"Did they hurt you?" she asked.

"No," said Dalton. "No, I'm fine."

"Come on, we gotta go!"

She pulled him out the door and looked up and down the side of the house. A blond woman, face in ruin, was rounding the corner from the front. Maylee figured she and Dalton could get around her. The backyard was too dark to chance.

"Wait!" said Dalton, pulling on her arm. "The phone! I forgot the phone!"

* * *

Brooke ran for the living room, hoping the corpses were following her. She stopped and looked back. Sure enough, they were stumbling after her, groaning and working their jaws. She looked around for a weapon. Nothing. Just toppled furniture, a ruined TV and ...

her phone!

She rushed over and bent to pick it up. She opened it and started punching in 911.

The corpses reached the living room. They came at her, groaning.

No time for phone calls. She closed the phone. "Guys!" she yelled, hoping Dalton and Maylee could hear. "Go out the kitchen door! I'm going out the front!"

She turned to rush out the front door. The pizza boy stood there, neck gaping and oozing dark blood. He gurgled and hissed at her.

Without thinking, without time for thought, Brooke backed away. Cold hands fell on her shoulders. She spun, screaming. The man with no eyes groaned at her. She wrenched herself free, backing away from the approaching group of corpses.

The pizza boy at her back grabbed her by the hair. He moaned and bit into the back of her head. Brooke sucked in a sharp gasp as his teeth scraped against her skull. Then pain hit and she shrieked.

She felt the pizza boy pull away a section of her scalp. She heard him chew. The corpses in front of her, led by the eyeless man, drew close. The eyeless man moaned and leaned in to bite her shoulder. Blood shot across the eyeless man's face, pooling in his empty eye sockets. Brooke screamed and the eyeless man chewed.

The other corpses drew near. Brooke was nearly lost in a haze of pain and shock. Her right hand still gripped her cell phone.

The kids.

She mustered the last bit of sanity and strength she had. She turned to face the pizza boy. He was chewing on a hunk of her scalp. Brooke saw her own hair and skin dangle from the pizza boy's mouth.

"Fuck you," she said. Then she flung the phone over his shoulder, out into the yard.

Please God, let them find it.

The eyeless man bit into her neck. Numerous cold hands closed on her.

Brooke screamed one last time.

* * *

"We have to get the phone!" said Dalton, pulling Maylee back toward the kitchen.

"Forget the phone!" yelled Maylee, tugging him back the other way. "We have to get out of here!"

"We gotta call Mom!" yelled Dalton, wriggling his hand free of Maylee and running back inside.

"Dammit, Dalton!" said Maylee. She gripped the handle of her bat and followed.

Maylee ran inside and first saw the broken-neck corpse stumbling blindly around. His face was still buried in his chest and he was far enough away to be safe for the moment. Dalton was grabbing the phone off its charger. He started dialing. Maylee ran over and snatched it from him.

"Forget the damned phone!" she said, dropping the phone on the counter. "We have to get out of here NOW."

Brooke's screams came from the living room. Both Maylee and Dalton stopped and looked at each other. The broken-neck corpse jerked in reaction to the scream, moaning into its chest and reaching at nothing.

"Brooke!" yelled Maylee, running through the kitchen and into the hallway. Dalton followed behind her.

The hallway was full of corpses, all pushing their way into the living room with their backs to Maylee and Dalton. Somewhere among them, Brooke was screaming. Maylee couldn't see her.

"Brooke!" Maylee shouted. She slammed the bat into the head of the closest corpse. The corpse shook and turned to face her. It was an old woman wearing a floral-print dress and a half-rotten old hat. Her eyes were white and she chattered brown, rotten teeth at Maylee.

Maylee screamed and the corpses clogging the hallway turned in response.

"Crap," said Dalton.

"Yeah," said Maylee. She turned to run back to the kitchen. Dalton followed.

Maylee stopped as she reached the kitchen. The blond woman missing the bottom half of her face was staggering in. Her bloody, ruined jaw worked up and down and she let out a bloody hiss.

Maylee gripped her bat tight and ran to the woman. Screaming, she slammed the woman across the head as hard as she could. The woman's head snapped to one side with a loud "pop" and the woman staggered. Maylee ran past her and into the side yard, assuming Dalton was behind her.

She was wrong. She spun around, looking. "Dalton?"

"Mom?" came Dalton's voice from the kitchen. "Mom, it's me!"

Maylee ran back into the kitchen. Dalton was at the counter, phone held to his ear.

"Dalton!" yelled Maylee. The corpses from the hallway were staggering into the kitchen. The two corpses already in the kitchen were staggering around, heads limp, but it was only a matter of time before one of them found him. Maylee rushed over and snatched the phone from Dalton's hand. "Dammit, we have to go!"

Mom's voice came from the phone, quiet and metallic sounding. "Maylee? Is that you?"

Maylee looked around the room. They had seconds to get out, maybe. She put the phone to her ear. "Mom?"

"Maylee?" came Mom's voice. "Oh thank God. Is there..."

"They're everywhere Mom, they just keep coming!"

"I know, honey. Just please get somewhere safe!"

Maylee looked around. It was going to be tight. "Mom, I'm sorry."

"What?"

Maylee swallowed. "I'm sorry for what I said, Mom." She sniffed and wiped at her eyes.

Dalton seemed to finally notice how close the corpses from the hallway were getting. He looked around, panic on his face.

"Maylee honey, I'm sorry too." It sounded like Mom was crying. "Just please..."

Dalton started screaming. Maylee looked around. The corpses were close now. One grabbed Dalton. He kept screaming, struggling with the corpse.

"Dalton!" yelled Maylee, dropping the phone.

"Maylee! Dalton!" came Mom's distant voice from the phone as it fell. Then Maylee was too far away to hear.

Eighteen

Angie clenched at the sound of her children screaming. She was pacing the patient hallway, cell phone against her ear. Park had given her the other rifle. It was slung over one shoulder, slapping against her back as she paced.

"Maylee!" she screamed into the phone. "Dalton!"

She heard the sounds of a struggle. And moaning. And her *children screaming.*

Then she heard something knocking the phone around. Feet? Hands? Her kids' hands?

"Maylee?" she yelled. Freeda ran in from the nurse's station.

"Dalton?" Angie yelled. Tears were coming freely now. She heard more screams, then the sound of something crunching down on the phone. Then static.

Then nothing. The phone was dead.

Angie stopped. She was at the far end of the hallway, in front of the window that looked out over the darkened trees and hills behind the hospital. She listened to the hum of her own phone.

"Maylee! Dalton!" she screamed. She was shaking. Her phone finally recognized the connection was lost and dropped it.

Angie was crying. "Oh god." She snapped the phone shut and let her hand fall to her side.

Then Freeda was behind her. "Anj?"

"They're dead, Freeda." Angie didn't look back at Freeda. She stared at the dark outlines of treetops. *Somewhere out there are more of the things that killed my children. Killed them while I was stuck in here.*

"You don't know that..."

"I heard it," said Angie. "Oh god, Freeda, I heard them screaming."

"Anj..."

"I wasn't there. Why the hell wasn't I there? My children died and I wasn't there."

Behind her, Freeda said nothing.

Angie drew in a ragged breath. "I can't do this anymore, Freeda."

"What do you mean?"

"I mean I'm done," Angie said, putting her forehead on the glass. *I could break out the window. I could jump.*

"Don't say things like that..."

"What the hell am I supposed to say?" said Angie, turning to face Freeda.

Sam Shuab grabbed Freeda from behind and bit into her temple.

Freeda gasped. Blood spurted from her temple and Sam chewed. His eyes were clouded and thick dark fluid oozed from the gaping hole in the back of his head.

"Freeda!" yelled Angie.

Sam pulled Freeda back down the hallway, chewing and moaning. Freeda grabbed at Angie but missed. Her arms flailed at nothing as Sam pulled her back. She kicked, her legs scraping against the floor.

Angie lunged forward, dropping her cell phone to the floor. She grabbed Freeda with both hands and tried to pull her away. Sam pulled back and bit deeper into Freeda's head. Freeda screamed. Blood ran down her face and into her open mouth. Her fingers dug into Angie's arm, strong at first but quickly becoming weaker.

Sam wrenched Freeda away from Angie like an animal protecting its food. He took several steps back, dragging Freeda with him. He kept chewing into Freeda's head. Freeda started shaking and convulsing.

Angie rushed after her. Her foot landed on her cell phone. She stumbled and heard her phone snap in two under her feet.

Angie stopped and watched Sam eating Freeda. Cold reason hit her. *It's too late.*

And only then did she remember the rifle on her back. *One more failure to add to the pile.*

She pulled the rifle from her shoulder and leveled it at Sam's forehead. How long had it been since she'd last handled a gun? She couldn't remember.

She remembered enough. She fired and Sam's head snapped back. Blood and bits of Freeda's head spilled from his mouth. He let go of Freeda and fell over backward.

Freeda slumped to the ground, twitching.

Angie stepped over and looked down at Freeda. Tears stung Angie's eyes and cheeks.

Freeda convulsed and jerked. Blood ran from her temple and onto the floor. Freeda looked at Angie. Pain and fear filled her eyes.

"Damn it," whispered Angie down at Freeda. "I'm sorry."

Angie pointed down and shot Freeda just above the left eye. A large red hole appeared in Freeda's head and Freeda slumped still.

"Oh god!" came Kristen's voice from the front of the hall. Angie looked. Kristen stood there, Park behind her. Mr. Paulson was out of sight somewhere behind them.

Kristen started to run in. Angie pointed the gun at her.

"Stop! All of you stop!"

"Oh god," said Kristen, shaking and putting her hands to her mouth. "I'm so sorry."

"You shut up! I should shoot you right now!"

"I couldn't do it," said Kristen. "Sam..."

Tears came faster now. "He was dead! I'm sorry for that, but he was already dead!" She motioned with the gun at Freeda's body. Her face still showed the fear and pain she had died in. "This didn't have to happen!"

She looked down at Freeda for several seconds. She drew in a breath and spun the gun around to face herself. She put the barrel in her mouth.

Kristen stepped forward. "No!"

Angie took the rifle out of her mouth and pointed it back at Kristen. "Stay back! There's nothing stopping me from shooting you first!"

Kristen was crying. "Your kids..."

"My kids are dead, you stupid bitch. And so am I."

She turned the rifle back on herself. She put her mouth over the barrel. It was still warm from shooting Freeda. She put her finger on the trigger.

The cell phone in Freeda's smock started ringing.

Angie stopped and stared at Freeda's pocket. She could see the phone flashing.

Kristen stood still at the front of the hall, biting the ends of her fingers.

The phone kept ringing.

Angie slowly removed the gun from her mouth and lowered it. She knelt down next to Freeda's body. Freeda stared at her with empty eyes. Angie fished the cell phone from Freeda's pocket. She opened it and answered.

"Hello?" she said.

"Mom?"

Maylee.

* * *

Maylee stood in the middle of the street just in front of what was left of her house. Dalton stood next to her, looking scared but unhurt. She held her bat in one hand and Brooke's cell phone in the other. She'd found it in the middle of the yard, where Brooke appeared to have thrown it. That or she made it out here, then went back into the house before ...

"Maylee?" said Mom's voice on the phone. "Oh my god. Are you okay? Is Dalton okay?"

"We're both fine. We tried calling your phone but it wouldn't answer. Finally I remembered Freeda's number. Brooke..." Maylee paused and swallowed.

When she and Dalton had escaped the kitchen, dropping the phone and ducking under the grasp of the corpses, their first thought had been to run around to the front of the house. That was the way Brooke had been running when they separated, and that was where Brooke's screaming had come from.

And that's where they had found what was left of Brooke. She had been torn open. Like a bag of meat and organs. And those things, those corpses that somehow still walked and ate, were crouching down next to her, pulling out hunks of her and eating. They had looked vacantly at Maylee and Dalton as they chewed.

"Why aren't they attacking us?" Dalton had asked.

"Because they already have food," Maylee had responded. "As soon as they run out, we'll be next."

Brooke's head had been the only recognizable part of her left. Her hair spread out toward the sidewalk. Her open eyes stared at Maylee and Dalton.

Maylee tried not to think of Brooke. Tried to focus on Mom's voice on the phone. "They got her, Mom."

"Oh my god," said Mom, quietly. "Listen, you have to get somewhere safe and hide."

"Nowhere's safe, Mom," said Maylee, walking up the street. She looked into the windows of the cars parked along the curb. Looking for something.

She found it.

"Maylee, you've got to..."

"Mom," said Maylee, cutting her off. "I have to confess something to you."

Mom paused. "What are you talking about?"

Maylee rubbed her hand on her forehead and looked up and down the street. She could hear screaming and see corpses wandering in the distance, but nothing close. The phone beeped in her ear. She held it away from her face and looked. The battery was dying. She sighed and put the phone back to her ear. "You know my friend Stacy? We've been sneaking out her mom's car from time to time. To practice driving."

"Maylee, you're fourteen!"

"I'm pretty sure I know that, Mom." She rolled her eyes at Dalton. He was looking up and down the street, looking scared. "And we don't have a lot of time right now, Brooke's phone's dying."

"You brought it up. Why on earth are we talking about this now?" asked Mom.

"Because someone left their keys in this car," said Maylee, looking through the window. "And we're stealing it."

"Maylee, you will do no such thing! The police..."

"Have more important things to worry about. We're coming to the hospital."

The phone beeped again and went dead.

* * *

Angie swore at the phone and dialed Brooke's number. It rang and rang, but no answer. Either Maylee was ignoring her or the phone had died like Maylee had said. She snapped the phone shut and walked to the nurse's station.

Kristen was standing there, red faced and crying. Park was standing with his arms crossed, rifle slung over his shoulder. Mr. Paulson sat in his wheelchair, scowling about something but keeping quiet.

"We going?" said Park.

"Yeah," said Angie. "We're going. We've got to get to the parking lot as soon as possible. My kids are alive and they're coming here."

"Oh thank god," said Kristen.

"You shut up," said Angie. "We're getting out, I'm getting my kids and we're getting the hell out of here."

"Works for me," said Park, shrugging. "Which way we going?"

"Pick a hallway," said Angie, taking the rifle from her shoulder and gripping it.

Nineteen

The corpses behind the glass doors writhed and grasped at them. Park stared at them, rifle slung over his shoulder. Why had he come back? What was he doing standing here with these people? He could have been dead by now.

"You sure guns will be enough?" asked Kristen, looking at Angie. "I'll have to push Dad."

"Glad someone thought of that," said Mr. Paulson.

Angie looked at Kristen, then Mr. Paulson. "Wait here." She slung the rifle over her shoulder and walked down the hallway. Park noticed she walked around Sam and Freeda but didn't look down.

"And what's on your deep ocean of a mind?" said Mr. Paulson.

"How much you'll slow me down," said Park.

Kristen scowled at him. Good. Last thing he wanted was anymore fucking friends.

It would be so easy to just blow his head off right now. Let them have one extra gun and one less person. Easy.

Angie walked back in, pushing an electric wheelchair. "Forgot we stored these in the back room."

Mr. Paulson snorted. "You mean I could have had one of those fuckers all this time?"

"Sure looks that way," said Angie. She pushed the chair until it was right next to Mr. Paulson.

"Here," she said, grabbing Mr. Paulson's arm. Kristen grabbed the other one and they helped Mr. Paulson over to the new chair.

Angie moved to switch the oxygen tank from one chair to the other. She glanced at Kristen, doting over her father. Kristen's face was red and taut. Full of anguish. Angie's face briefly softened, but the look was quickly gone. *Damn right,* thought Park. *Stupid bitch got her friend killed.*

The tank done, Angie stepped over to the front of the wheelchair. "Push the button here," she said, pointing.

"I know how to do it," said Mr. Paulson, pushing her hand away. He pushed a button on the right arm of the chair and the joystick-like controller lit up. He pulled the controller back and the chair lurched backward, almost hitting Kristen.

"Whoopsie-daisy," said Kristen, her voice raw and flat. She laughed but her eyes weren't in it. Park considered offering to shoot her, but he chuckled and looked away.

"What's so funny?" said Angie.

"Nothing," said Park. "Can we go anytime soon?"

"Damn," said Kristen, looking at her hands. Black grease from the wheelchair's underside was smeared across her fingers.

"Better wash those," said Angie. "Don't want to drop anything once we're out there."

Kristen walked over to the sink and turned on the hot water. It sputtered, spit out a few drops, then stopped. Kristen turned on the cold. Nothing.

"What's wrong?" said Angie, walking over. Park followed, curious.

"Great, just great," said Kristen, wiping her hands on her shirt. She sniffed and rubbed at one of her eyes. Black smeared across her cheek. "The water's out."

"Something must have happened to the main," said Park. "All kinds of shit going on out there, it's a wonder the lights haven't gone off for good yet."

Angie nodded. "Wait, if the water's off..." She looked around at the ceiling. "Give me your lighter."

"I'm out of cigarettes," said Park. "Can't help you there."

"Just the lighter," Angie said, not taking her eyes off the ceiling.

Park shrugged. He fished out his lighter and handed it to her.

Angie walked over to the nurse's desk and climbed up onto it.

"What the holy fuck are you doing up there?" said Mr. Paulson, wheeling himself over. "I thought dumbshit there broke the ladder. And besides, how would I..."

"Now, Dad," said Kristen, walking over to him. "Let's just see what she's doing." She sounded upbeat but her voice was shaking.

Angie flicked the lighter on and held it up to the nearest sprinkler. The sprinkler sputtered out a few drops but otherwise did not respond.

Angie smiled. "If the water's off, then so are the sprinklers." She tossed the lighter back to Park, then jumped down off the desk. "And you said they don't like fire, right?"

Park nodded. "Yeah, but we've just got the one lighter."

"Two," said Mr. Paulson, fishing an old-fashioned butane lighter from his hospital robe.

"Dad!" said Kristen. "What do you have that for?"

"I use it to warm my balls, what the hell do you think?" said Mr. Paulson.

Park looked at Mr. Paulson, then back to Angie. "Okay then, two. Now we have twice the amount of jack shit we had before."

"Wait here," said Angie, walking over to the sink. She opened some cabinets and started rooting around.

Park looked over at Kristen and Mr. Paulson. Kristen was doting and Mr. Paulson was sulking.

It would be so easy to shoot himself. But he wanted to see what Angie had planned.

Angie pulled out a plastic jug of something. Then two more. Then three more. She took one of the jugs and carried it over.

"Rubbing alcohol," she said. "Won't burn for long but it will burn. Watch."

She took Park's lighter from his hand without asking. She walked over to one of the glass doors. Corpses writhed and bit at her. She splashed some of the alcohol on the door and lit it. Flame roared across the glass for a few seconds, then was gone. The glass was scorched and darkened and the room smelled of smoke. But behind the glass, the corpses had backed up several feet.

Park raised an eyebrow and nodded. "That would definitely help."

Angie nodded back at him. She held out his lighter. Park shook his head. "Keep it. You start fires, I'll shoot." He smirked at her.

She smirked back and put the lighter in her smock pocket. "Okay then. Let's see what else we have we can use as weapons."

Mr. Paulson pointed at the jugs of alcohol. "I hope you aren't planning on me carrying all those fuckers."

Angie looked down at Mr. Paulson, then reached for his waist.

"What the fuck?" said Mr. Paulson. Angie grabbed the belt of his hospital robe and pulled it free.

"Hospital property," she said. She walked over to the jugs of alcohol. She threaded the belt through four of the jug handles, then lifted it all up off the counter. She tied the belt around her waist, two jugs dangling at each hip. She double knotted and pulled it so tight Park winced.

"That's gotta hurt," said Park.

"You bet it does," said Angie. "But it'll work."

Park nodded. "Got anything sharp? Scalpels or some shit?"

Angie thought about it, then walked to another counter. She pulled open a drawer and pulled out packets of scalpels and blades. She opened the protective plastic and put four scalpels together. She stuck one in the robe belt. She handed the other three out to Park, Kristen and Mr. Paulson.

"They don't feel pain," said Angie, "but you can use these to cut free a finger or hand. Wish we had something that could cut deeper, but surgeries aren't generally done at the nurse's station."

Angie paused, looking at Kristen. "Here," she said. She took the rifle off her shoulder and handed it to her. "Since Mr. Paulson can move himself now, you can use this."

Kristen blanched at the sight of the gun. "I'm not really that good with a gun..."

Angie cut her off. "You were good enough to pretend to shoot Sam. Just take it. Aim for the brain and try not to waste ammo."

Kristen took the gun.

Angie turned to look at the three glass doors. The corpses had returned to the scorched one. All three doors were covered with corpses, squirming and grasping. Park stepped up next to her.

"Which door?" he said, taking his rifle off his shoulder.

Angie shrugged. She picked up a fifth jug of alcohol and popped off the cap. She took out the lighter. "I don't suppose it matters." She pointed at the one in the middle. "Though that one will give us a choice of two hallways at the middle of it. It splits off. One half goes straight to the emergency room. That's the hallway we came down to get here. The other half goes to the cafeteria, laundry room, and eventually back around to just outside the emergency room."

"Always good to have choices," said Park. "I guess we'll do that one."

Angie turned to the others. "We ready?"

Twenty

Maylee frowned down at Brooke's phone. The display complained of low battery, then winked out completely. It was dead. "Guess we won't be going back to the house to see if Brooke brought the charger with her."

Dalton looked back at the house, then back at Maylee. "They had her insides, Maylee." He had a look Maylee hadn't seen on him since he was very small.

"I know," said Maylee, pushing down her own fear. "But we just have to try not to think about it. Let's get this car and get to Mom, okay?"

Dalton looked down, then back up. "Do you think... do you think I got Brooke killed?"

Maylee bit her lip and looked at him. "No, Dalton." She knelt to look him in the eye. "Listen to me. Those things are what killed Brooke. We were just trying to get the phone so we could call for help. Okay?"

Dalton looked at her. For a second he was a scared little kid. Then the braver Dalton, the Dalton who had knocked a hole to the basement and crawled through it, resurfaced. "Okay."

She smiled at him. "Now, let's steal a car."

She stood. Dalton looked up and down the street. "Won't we get in trouble?"

Maylee shrugged. "Maybe. But I think there's more important things to worry about."

"Brooke has ...*had* a car."

Maylee looked at him. "You want to go back to get the keys from her?"

Dalton looked back to the house, then back to Maylee. He shook his head.

"Me neither," she said. She turned back to the car and pulled on the door handle. "Damn."

"What?" said Dalton.

"It's locked. Whoever's car this is must have locked their keys in the car."

"Should we find another one?"

Maylee looked up and down the street. She could hear moaning, this time a little closer than before. "Don't think we'll get lucky like this again. And besides, we have to get moving. Can't stay in one place very long tonight."

"Those corpses are everywhere," said Dalton.

"Yeah," said Maylee. "Stand back." She took a step back from the car and swung her bat at the driver's window. It shattered with a loud crash, sending glass to the street and all across the front seat of the car.

Dalton walked up, wide-eyed. "Damn. It's your fault if I get glass in my butt."

"Just get in." She reached inside and hit the unlock button.

Dalton went to the other side and opened the door. Maylee opened the driver's door and brushed as much glass as she could out into the street. She tossed her bat in the back seat and sat, wincing at the sound of crunching glass but feeling no pain that would indicate injury.

"Okay," she said. "This should work. Put on your seat belt."

"What? We're stealing a car, Maylee. Car thieves don't need to wear seat belts."

She turned to glare at him. "Will you just do it?" She fastened hers. "I'm not going to get us this far and then kill us both in a crash."

Grumbling, he fastened his seat belt. "I wonder why the person whose car this was left their keys in it."

Maylee shrugged. "Probably rushing to get inside. Probably heard about all the trouble on the news."

"What if he died in the car?"

Maylee rolled her eyes at him. "If he died in the car, he'd still be sitting in the front seat. Dead people don't move."

They both looked at each other, realizing.

A corpse grabbed at them from the back seat.

Maylee and Dalton both screamed. The corpse, a thin man in a business suit, clutched Maylee's head and pulled back. Maylee frantically scrambled with the seat belt latch. The thin man pulled Maylee's cheek close to his mouth. The seat belt came free. Maylee grabbed the hard metal end of the strap and shoved it into the man's eye. He made no reaction.

Dalton was struggling with his seat belt. Maylee balled up her hand and slammed backward at where the seat belt was lodged in the corpse's eye. She heard something pop and the corpse let go and seemed to lose focus. *I must have hurt the brain.*

"Dalton!" she said, twisting in the seat to help him with the seat belt. "The brain! You've got to hurt the brain to stop these things." She undid his belt and he slid out the passenger door.

She opened her door and jumped outside. Dalton ran around to her side of the car. "My bat?" Maylee said. "Where's my bat?"

"You left it in the back seat," said Dalton. He tugged at her hand. "Come on. Let's just go."

Maylee shook her head. The corpse was thrashing around in the back seat, sluggishly and slow, but still dangerous. "No. We need this car to get to Mom."

She reached back inside the open driver's door, around to the back seat. The corpse was thrashing just a few feet away, so she moved quick. She pulled up the lock on the driver's side rear door. Then she hurriedly grabbed her bat and pulled her arm back. Looking around the pavement, she found a fallen tree branch and tossed it to Dalton. The she stepped back, holding the bat.

"Now, go unlock the other door."

"What? No way."

"Come on, Dalton!" She looked up and down the street. "We don't have much time."

"What's the stick for?"

"To push him out this side," said Maylee, using the bat to indicate her side.

"You're nuts!"

"Will you just do it!"

Dalton grumbled as he walked around and opened the passenger front door. He looked through the window at the corpse. The corpse was closer to Maylee's side and seemed not to notice Dalton at all. He reached in very carefully, and quickly pulled up the lock on the passenger rear door. He drew his hand out quickly and stepped away from the car.

"Dammit! That thing could have bit me."

"I know," said Maylee. "But you did good. Now open the door."

"Maylee..."

"Dalton, hurry! Those things are wandering around everywhere and we have no idea when one's gonna find us out here. Maybe even a bunch of them. We have to get in this car."

Dalton made a very worried whine and opened the back door.

Maylee opened hers. The corpse heard the sound and whipped its head from side to side, grunting. The seat belt fell from the corpse's eye.

"Now push!" said Maylee.

Dalton steeled himself and shoved the corpse in the shoulder with the branch. The corpse toppled out of the car onto the pavement, right at Maylee's feet.

It had just started to right itself when Maylee slammed her bat down on the corpse's skull. There was a horrible "crack" and the thing moaned.

Dalton came around to Maylee's side, mouth hanging open, watching Maylee.

"Dammit," said Maylee, slamming the bat down again. The corpse's head crumpled and blood seeped out a crack in its forehead. But it still moved, grabbing weakly at her.

"Just fucking die!" she screamed, slamming down one more time. The corpse's skull collapsed and Maylee's bat rang off the pavement. The corpse was still.

"Crap," said Dalton, looking down.

Maylee panted down at her handiwork. "We're gonna have to get something better than a bat." She looked at the blood and flesh coating her bat and grimaced. She wiped it on the corpse's clothes.

"That's gross, Maylee," said Dalton.

"Well I'm sorry. Do you have a hanky on you?"

"No."

"Then shut up." She checked the bat again. It was clean. "Let's get out of here."

She shut the back door on her side and Dalton went around and did his. They both climbed back in the car and shut the front doors. Maylee wiped her seat belt on the seat, then put it back on.

"The seat belt again?" said Dalton.

"Just do it."

He sighed and did.

Maylee let out a long sigh and turned the ignition.

Nothing. Not the slightest attempt at starting.

"What's wrong?" said Dalton.

Maylee tried a few more times, then groaned. "Oh shit. The dead guy must have died with the car running. The gas is gone, Dalton." She pulled the keys out and sat back in the seat.

Dalton took off his seat belt. "Looks like we're walking."

"For now," said Maylee, undoing hers. "I'll think of something." She climbed out of the car and the corpse of a woman hissed at her, inches from her face.

Maylee screamed. The woman's brown hair was matted with blood and her eyes rolled back into her head. The woman leaned in to bite.

With a grunt, Dalton came running around the other side of the car and shoved the woman down. The woman fell to the pavement, squirming and moaning.

"Hurry!" said Dalton, pointing at her. "Bat her!"

Maylee shook herself out of her shock. "Oh, right." She reached back into the car and grabbed the bat.

The woman was sitting back up and groaning just as Maylee slammed the woman across the cheek. The woman's jaw split and blood flew off to one side.

"The brain!" said Dalton.

"I know! I'm the one who told you!" said Maylee. She brought the bat over her head and slammed downward as hard as she could. The top of the woman's head bent inward. Blood seeped out her ears. She fell backward and was still.

"Dammit!" said Maylee. She wiped sweat from her forehead. "This is why I told you we have to hurry." She wiped the bat on the woman's clothes, noticing the woman was wearing pajamas and a bathrobe.

Dalton noticed it too. "She must have come from the house."

Maylee nodded. "Yeah, probably." She looked up and down the street, still winded. "Okay, let's go."

She and Dalton started walking toward the end of the street. Then she stopped.

"Wait," she said, looking at the keys in her hand.

"What?" said Dalton, turning back.

"There's a bunch of keys on here, and two car unlocker-things," said Maylee, showing Dalton the key chain.

Dalton walked back to her and looked. "So? Maybe that was his wife there, and that's the thing to her car."

Maylee nodded. "Yeah. And do you know what this is?" She indicated a small device hanging from one end of the chain.

"No. What?"

Maylee pointed the device toward the house and clicked it. With a whine and a squeaking of gears, the garage to the house's left opened. The door slowly rose up and shuddered to a stop.

Another car sat in the garage.

"Please work, please work, please work," said Maylee, pointing the key chain at the new car and pushing one of the unlock buttons.

The car beeped and lit up.

Maylee turned back to Dalton and grinned.

Twenty-One

Angie stared at the corpses behind the door. The room would be full of them in seconds once they opened the door.

"Everyone sure they're ready?" she said. "We'll have to move quick."

"Yep," said Park, holding his rifle.

Kristen said nothing, but held her rifle as well. Mr. Paulson was quiet for the moment, hand on the wheelchair controller.

Angie looked back at Park. "You think this will work?"

Park shrugged. "Hope so."

Angie turned back to the door. "Yeah. Me too."

The corpses bit at the glass.

"Okay," she said. "Let's go."

Angie splashed the door with rubbing alcohol and lit it. Flame shot across the glass for a few seconds, then sputtered out. The glass was blackened and the corpses behind it had backed up several feet. Angie unlocked the door quickly and opened it.

The corpses groaned and came for them.

"Everyone back up!" yelled Angie. They all stepped backward, further into the room.

Corpses filed in, groaning and biting at them. The group stayed clear, backing up as more corpses entered the room.

"This won't work," said Kristen. "Oh god. This isn't going to work."

"Shut the fuck up," said Park.

"Circle back!" said Angie.

The group turned, backing up to their left now. More corpses came in. There were at least twenty in the room now. They reached for the group as they came in, but were blocked by the nurse's desk. Angie and Park had pushed the nurse's desk so that it ran outward from the door frame, corralling the corpses straight into the room. A few more came through, then no more.

"That must be it for the immediate hallway," said Angie. "Everyone keep backing up!"

The group backed toward the wall now. The desk was at their left. Some of the corpses stumbled around the desk and moved toward them.

"I think now would be a good time," said Park.

"Yeah," said Angie. She climbed up onto the desk and stood. Taking the open jug of alcohol, she dumped a large amount on the floor just by the door. A few corpses, the last to enter the room, reached for her but missed.

Angie set the jug down and knelt on the desk. Leaning forward with the lighter, she lit the puddle she had made.

Flame wooshed up at her and into the room. She pulled back, nearly singed. The corpses moaned and backed further away from the door, deeper into the room.

"Now!" yelled Angie, jumping from the desk and back to the others. She and Park pushed the desk to the other side of the door, right over the already-sputtering flame. The corpses were still backing away, moaning and wincing at the fire.

"Hurry!" said Angie. Kristen and Mr. Paulson rushed out the door and into the hallway. Angie and Park moved to the far side of the desk and pushed it against the door, blocking it. They both climbed over the desk and out the door.

Angie shut the door, looking at the corpses filling the nurse's station. Freeda's body was still in there, but she pushed the thought down. There was no helping that.

"Too bad these don't lock from the outside," said Angie.

"The desk should slow them down pretty good," said Park, turning to look down the hallway.

"Yeah," Angie nodded.

A moan came from further down the hall. The rest of the group turned to look. A corpse, a man with a missing ear and arm, was stumbling toward them.

"Hey fuckface," said Park. "You missed the party in the room back there."

Park leveled the rifle at the corpse and fired. The corpse's head snapped back and it dropped to the floor.

"Not bad," said Angie.

"Yeah," said Park. "If only deer would walk as slow as these things."

"And if only you two talked as little as they do," said Mr. Paulson. "Are we going or what?"

"This way," said Angie, walking down the hallway. "Follow me."

They moved quickly and quietly down the hall. Angie's back strained under the weight of the alcohol jugs tied to her waist. The whir of Mr. Paulson's wheelchair was the only sound.

Each of the patient rooms they passed was empty. Blood and hunks of meat were scattered across the beds, across floors and across the walls. But nothing moving. Nothing biting.

"So far, so good," Angie muttered.

They passed a room and Angie glanced inside. A patient was hanging sideways off the bed. A large hole had been chewed into their head. Brain and bloody muck coated the sheets.

They had cleared the room, Mr. Paulson bringing up the rear, when a corpse burst through the door.

"Shit!" said Mr. Paulson. The corpse was an old man in a cowboy hat. Portions of his cheek were missing, and flaps of bloody skin dangled as he moved.

The man grabbed Mr. Paulson. Mr. Paulson wrenched at the joystick and the wheelchair sped backward. The man held on, dragging alongside the chair. The man's teeth inched toward Mr. Paulson's face.

"Someone get this fucker off me!" Mr. Paulson yelled.

"Dad!" yelled Kristen, racing after him.

"Dammit, dumbass!" yelled Park. "Use your gun!"

"Dad!" Kristen kept running, holding her gun in one hand and showing no sign of using it.

"Shit," said Park. He leveled the gun at the chair and fired.

Kristen screamed and dropped to her knees. Mr. Paulson's chair stopped. The corpse shook, then slid to the floor. Blood oozed from under the corpse's hat.

"You crazy fucker!" said Mr. Paulson, wheeling the chair further back, away from the corpse.

"Dad!" said Kristen, climbing to her feet and rushing over. "Are you okay?"

"Of course I'm okay," said Mr. Paulson. "No thanks to you three." He wheeled around her and back to Angie and Park. Kristen followed.

Angie watched them approach and sighed. Kristen looked shaken, but Angie refused to feel sorry for her. *Not yet.* "I gave you the gun for a reason," she said.

Kristen looked at the gun in her hand and frowned. "Sorry."

"Don't be sorry," Angie said, turning back to head down the hall. "Just be smart." She started walking. The others followed.

Things were quiet for several more feet. Angie held up a hand and the others stopped. A few feet up ahead, another hallway split off to the right. And many feet ahead of that, several corpses had stumbled out of their rooms, groaning. The corpses hadn't noticed them yet.

"Wait here," Angie whispered.

"Fuck that," whispered Park. He turned back to Kristen and Mr. Paulson. "You two wait here."

Angie and Park crept toward the opening of the side hallway.

"This the second hallway you talked about?" whispered Park. The corpses up ahead continued to ignore them.

"Yeah," whispered Angie. "And it looks like we might have to use it. Unless there's even more of those things down there."

They reached the edge of the opening and slowly peered around it.

The second hall was empty.

"Looks good to me," whispered Park.

"Yeah," whispered Angie, casting a glance at the corpses further down to their left. They still hadn't noticed. "It's just a longer way around. We'll have to move even faster. I've got to be outside when my kids get here."

Park nodded.

"Hey!" yelled Mr. Paulson. "Are we fucking moving in here?"

Angie and Park turned back to Mr. Paulson. Kristen whispered to him. "Dad, we've got to be quiet."

"For fuck's sake," said Mr. Paulson, loudly. "You all retarded? Those things are dead. They can't hear."

The corpses down the hall moaned and started moving toward them.

Mr. Paulson blinked. "Well, fuck me."

"Yeah," said Park.

"Come on," said Angie, starting down the side hallway. Park followed her.

They moved quickly for a few feet before Angie realized Kristen and Mr. Paulson weren't following.

"Wait," said Angie, stopping. She turned and trotted back to the main hall.

Mr. Paulson was struggling with his chair. Kristen was trying to help. The corpses were closing in, getting close to where Angie stood, leaning out into the hallway.

"What's wrong?" said Angie, running over.

"Fucking chair's broken!" said Mr. Paulson, wrenching the joystick from one side to the other.

"Careful, Dad," said Kristen. "Don't break it."

"It's already fucking broken, idiot!" yelled Mr. Paulson.

Park came back into the hallway. He looked at the three at the chair, then at the corpses coming closer. "We gotta move!" he said. He fired down the hallway, taking down one of the approaching corpses.

Angie moved to the back of the wheelchair. Mr. Paulson cursed and wrenched at the joystick. The corpses groaned and drew nearer.

"Wait," said Angie. "A wire came off the battery. It must have come loose earlier."

Mr. Paulson wrenched the joystick from one side to the other. "Damn it! Those fucking things are getting closer!"

"Your fault, dipshit!" said Park, firing at another corpse. The corpse went into a spasm then fell, limp. Three were left, getting close now. Soon they would block the way to the side hall. Park backed up, reloading the rifle.

"Hold on," said Angie, taking hold of the loose wire and moving it back to the battery.

Park finished loading the rifle and shot down another corpse. Two were left. "We don't have unlimited ammo here! I was only able to grab a few boxes!"

Mr. Paulson swore and leaned on the joystick.

Park fired again. One corpse was left, a large man with bloody, matted hair.

Angie snapped the wire connector into place on the battery.

The wheelchair sprung to life and shot down the hallway. "Shit!" yelled Mr. Paulson. The chair collided with Park, knocking him forward. Park sprawled to the floor, spinning to face up, toward the corpse. The corpse groaned and reached down at him. Park tried to move his rifle into position but the corpse knocked it aside in its blind grasping.

The corpse groaned and opened its mouth.

A shot rang out. The corpse's head snapped to one side and its body shook. Then it fell over, off of Park and onto the floor.

Angie looked to see Kristen lowering her rifle.

"Shit!" said Park, standing. He kicked the wheel of Mr. Paulson's chair. "Be fucking careful or you'll be dragging your crippled ass!"

"Hey!" yelled Kristen, pointing the rifle at Park. "You leave my father alone!"

Park scowled at her.

More groans came from the far end of the hall. Another group of corpses came into view.

Angie pushed Kristen's gun down and addressed Park. "We gotta go."

Kristen pulled her gun away from Angie's hand but kept it down. "Keep your friend away from my father."

Angie looked at Kristen. "My friend is half eaten in the nurse's station."

She turned away from Kristen and Mr. Paulson and headed for the side hall. Park raised his eyebrows at her as she passed.

She stopped at the entrance and looked down the second hallway. Still clear, as far as she could tell. "Okay," she said, looking back to the others. "Let's hurry."

Twenty-Two

Maylee looked quickly up and down the street. "Come on," she said. "Let's go."

She ran to the open garage, Dalton behind her. The car sat inside, the running lights casting the garage in a dim glow.

"Wait," said Dalton, stopping behind her.

Maylee stopped and turned. "What?"

Dalton was staring at the garage. "I thought I heard something in there."

Maylee turned back to look. She saw nothing. The running lights switched off and the garage fell back into darkness. She listened. She still heard moans, far away but getting closer, but nothing coming from the garage.

"It's fine," said Maylee, gripping her bat. "Come on." She raised up the keys and clicked the unlock button again.

The running lights came back on.

Something lunged at them from under the car.

They both screamed and jumped back. Maylee dropped the keys and raised her bat with both hands.

A small and very startled mouse blinked at her and ran down the street.

Maylee watched it go for a moment, then let out her breath and lowered the bat. "Dammit."

"They had mice, too," said Dalton, also watching the mouse.

"Probably had the same landlord," said Maylee. Her heart was pounding. She reached down to the pavement and recovered the keys. "Now hurry up and get in the car."

Maylee ran into the garage and grabbed the driver's side door handle. She pulled open the door. She cast a look in the back seat, just in case. Nothing. She tossed the bat back there and climbed into the driver's seat. Dalton climbed in the passenger seat. They both shut their doors.

"Okay," said Maylee.

"You sure you can drive?" said Dalton.

"Sure I can do it better than you," said Maylee. She tried putting a key in the ignition. It didn't fit. She sighed and tried another one. It didn't fit either.

"You need the key that starts the car," said Dalton.

"Be quiet, Dalton," said Maylee. Finally she found a key that fit.

She was about to turn it when a corpse stumbled into view.

They both gasped.

The corpse was wandering down the street, passing in front of the open garage door.

"Be quiet," whispered Maylee, staring at the corpse. "It hasn't heard us."

She heard movement from Dalton's seat and looked. He was pulling the bat from the back seat.

"Leave that alone," Maylee whispered. "Just keep quiet and let the thing walk past."

"I want it just in case," whispered Dalton, clutching the bat and staring out the window. The corpse was halfway across the open garage door.

"It's mine, anyway," whispered Maylee, grabbing the bat. "Give it to me."

Dalton pulled back. "No," he whispered.

"Dammit, Dalton," Maylee whispered. They tugged the bat back and forth. Maylee pulled hard. Dalton scowled at her and pulled back. Maylee shifted in her seat and her elbow hit the car horn.

The horn blared out of the garage onto the street.

"Shit," said Maylee, letting go of the bat.

The corpse grunted and looked their direction. Two other corpses came around the corner. All three began to move toward the car.

"Double shit," said Maylee, grabbing the keys and turning.

"Hurry!" said Dalton.

The car came to life. The corpses were close to the garage now. Maylee tried to put her foot on the gas, then discovered the seat was too far back.

"Shit," she said, reaching down for the seat lever. She could hear the corpses groaning now.

She pulled the seat up further and straightened back up. The corpses were in the garage.

"Hurry, Maylee!" yelled Dalton.

Maylee pulled down the gear shift and slammed on the gas.

The car rocketed backward and slammed into the garage wall. Maylee and Dalton were thrown back in their seats.

"Ow!" yelled Dalton.

"Dammit!" said Maylee, fumbling with the gear shift.

The corpses were closing in on the car.

Maylee moved the shifter into drive and gave the car gas. The wheels spun but the car didn't move.

"Why aren't we moving?" said Dalton, staring at the corpses and clutching the bat tightly.

"We're stuck on something!" said Maylee, pushing harder on the gas. The wheels spun and she smelled smoke. The corpses reached the car. They grabbed at the hood and groaned.

"Crap!" yelled Dalton.

Maylee screamed and slammed all her weight on the gas. The tires screeched but the car stayed put.

"Dammit!" yelled Maylee, slamming her weight down in the seat. The car bounced. She heard something behind the car clatter and the tires engaged. The car shot forward, knocking the corpses aside.

The car bounced onto the street and kept going. Maylee and Dalton screamed as the car raced across the street and into a mailbox on the other side. The mailbox flew across the yard and smashed against the wall of the house behind it.

Maylee finally took her foot off the gas. She was panting. She looked in the rearview mirror. The corpses were strewn in the street, beaten up but still moving. One of them was almost to its feet.

"Damn, Maylee," said Dalton. "You sure you drive better than me?"

"Yes," said Maylee. She put the car in reverse and backed into the street. The car bounced as it hit the pavement. She spun backward until the car was facing the right way. "Now put on your seat belt."

"Seriously?" Dalton raised his eyebrows at her.

"Dammit, Dalton, just put on the shitting seat belt right shitting now!" Maylee yelled, sounding a little like Mom when Mom was really, *really* mad.

Dalton glared at her and clicked his seat belt into place.

"Thank you," said Maylee, then put on her own seat belt. "Now we can go."

She put the car into drive and drove.

Twenty-Three

Angie entered the laundry room, Park right behind her. Kristen and Mr. Paulson followed. One of the dryers was still running, loud and hot. Stacks of linens were piled everywhere.

Mr. Paulson looked around. "You people actually wash these things? Shit, how dirty were they before?"

"Be quiet," said Angie. She walked to the other side of the room, where another door led back out into the hall. She looked carefully around the edge of the door. Nothing.

"Okay," she said, walking back to the others. "It's clear for the moment. Let's get our shit together and then get back to it."

She walked to a folding counter and set her jug of alcohol on it. *Freeda had been folding sheets at this table.* She undid the belt around her waist and took one of the full jugs from the belt. She used the full jug to refill the used one. Then she slid the jug back onto the belt and tied the belt around her waist.

Park was reloading his rifle. He shook the box of ammo and cursed. "Running kind of low already."

"Great," said Mr. Paulson. "So we'll all get halfway, then run out of ammo and get eaten. What a great fucking plan this is."

Park looked at Mr. Paulson. The large dryer in the corner rumbled and groaned.

"Well, here's a thought," said Park. "How about you keep your fucking mouth shut and quit attracting their fucking attention?"

Kristen sighed, looking at both Park and Mr. Paulson. "We aren't getting out of here, are we?"

"Quit saying crap like that," said Angie, adjusting her belt.

"Sam died before we even got out of that room. How in the hell are we going to make it all the way out of this building?"

"I said quit saying crap like that!" Angie snapped, glaring at Kristen.

Kristen sighed again and backed up against a wall. She put her head back.

Angie gave her one more glare, then went back to adjusting her belt.

The dryer stopped.

The groaning didn't.

Angie spun around to face the dryer. Park turned his rifle to it.

"What the hell's that noise?" said Mr. Paulson.

The groaning could be heard clearly now. It was not mechanical. It was loud and gurgling. From what sounded like a choking throat.

Angie looked more closely at the dryer. It was set a foot or so away from the wall.

"Shit," she said. "It's behind the dryer."

"Well, it's stuck then," said Park. "Let's leave it and get the fuck out of here."

"Wait," said Angie. "We can't be sure. It could be someone hiding."

"They're awfully fucking small," said Park.

"And not very verbal," said Mr. Paulson.

"It could be a hurt child," said Kristen. "A survivor. Hurt and hiding."

Angie looked at Kristen and nodded. She hated her, but she was right.

"We have to make sure it's dead before we leave it," said Angie.

"Fine," said Park. "Just hurry."

Angie stepped toward the dryer. The groaning continued. It did indeed sound like a child's voice.

"Is someone there?" said Angie, taking another step.

The groan became louder. Whatever was behind the dryer gurgled and moaned.

"It's okay. We're friends." She stepped up to the edge of the dryer. "Don't be scared." She looked over at Park. Park nodded and got his rifle ready.

Angie nodded to Park and turned back to the dryer. She took a breath and pulled the dryer further away from the wall. She leaned over the top of the dryer, looking down.

Two small, cold hands grabbed her face and pulled.

"Fuck!" Angie heard Park say behind her.

"That's it," said Mr. Paulson. "She's done. Let's get out of here!" Angie heard the wheelchair start to whir.

Angie looked down at what had grabbed her. A small child, hungry and very obviously dead. It was a small boy with portions of his scalp chewed away. He tugged at Angie's head but was not strong enough to get his writhing mouth to her.

"Oh shit," said Angie, softly. It was the boy. The boy Angie had seen eaten.

"Stop right fucking there!" yelled Park, presumably at Mr. Paulson.

The wheelchair stopped. "You gonna pull a gun on a crippled old man?" said Mr. Paulson.

"Stop pointing that thing at my father!" yelled Kristen. Angie heard Kristen's gun cock.

Angie felt tears coming. The boy writhed and gnashed at her. His fingers pawed at her face, but he was too weak to do any damage. "I'm sorry," she said.

She pulled her face away and turned to the others. Park had his rifle pointed at Mr. Paulson. Kristen had her rifle pointed at Park. "Knock it the fuck off!" Angie said, stomping over to Kristen. She snatched the rifle away.

"Back off, bitch!" said Kristen, tears in her eyes. "His stupid friend killed my husband!"

"Shut the fuck up or I will shoot you myself," said Angie, stepping back over to the boy. The boy was still caught behind the dryer, but his head and arms were now visible over the top.

Angie stared at the boy and allowed herself a few seconds to cry.

"Who the fuck is that?" asked Park.

"I dunno," said Angie. "Just some kid, I guess." She swallowed, leveled the rifle and fired.

The boy's head rocked and a large hole appeared in his forehead. His glazed eyes closed and he slumped forward. Dark blood slowly pooled on the top of the dryer.

She turned and gave the rifle back to Kristen. "This is only for those things." She looked at Park. "Same goes for you. Now come on, we've made enough noise."

Groans came from both doorways.

"Dammit!" said Park.

Angie looked in both directions. Corpses were already stumbling in the way they had come. The groans from the way out were getting closer. She scanned the room quickly.

"This is it!" yelled Park. "Just keep shooting until the ammo runs out."

"Then what?" said Kristen as she looked around, panic on her face.

"Then I finally get my wish," said Park, quietly. Angie was close enough to hear. She ignored it for the time being.

Her eyes landed on a wheeled cart full of folded white linen. "Here," she said, running over to the cart. She opened the jug of alcohol and dumped all of it onto the linen.

More corpses from the way they had come groaned and came through the doorway. Angie took out Park's lighter and lit the pile of linens. It burst instantly into flames.

"Shit!" said Mr. Paulson.

Angie screamed and pushed the cart into the corpses. The corpses moaned as the cart hit them. The corpses and most of the doorway burst into flame.

"Crazy bitch!" yelled Mr. Paulson. "We're flammable too!"

"Not if we run," said Angie, turning for the second door. "Go!"

All four of them moved to the door. Three corpses came through the other way, blocking them.

"Shit!" said Park, raising the rifle.

Angie was out in front, inches from the closest corpse. The corpse, what was left of a dried rotted woman covered in a dirty burial dress, grabbed her. The woman's mouth opened, dry skin ripping and cracking, and she leaned in to bite. Angie fumbled in her smock, found the scalpel, and shoved it into the woman's eye socket. Angie grunted and pushed the scalpel in as hard as she could. The corpse shook, then dropped away from her.

"Duck!" yelled Park.

Angie did. Park's rifle went off, the shot flying over Angie's head and into the corpse standing closest to her.

"Shoot the other one!" she yelled. The remaining corpse, a man covered in yellow and red sores, fell on her, groaning. She rolled over on to her back, trying to push him up. He was heavy and strong.

"I can't get a shot!" yelled Park.

"Leave her!" yelled Mr. Paulson.

Fire was spreading on the far wall. Angie could feel the heat from it. She put her palm on the corpse's forehead. He snarled and bit at her, missing but close. Angie pushed upward with all her might. The corpse's head moved up an inch or two, but that was all.

"You'll have to do better than that!" yelled Park.

"Fuck the stupid bitch!" yelled Mr. Paulson. "We're going to burn to death if we stay!"

Angie heard Mr. Paulson's wheelchair start to move. She heard it whir toward the door. From the corner of her vision, she saw one of his wheels move past her.

"Get back here!" yelled Park.

The wheel of Mr. Paulson's chair crunched over the leg of the corpse atop Angie. "Shit!" said Mr. Paulson, trying to swing the chair the other direction. He connected with the corpse's thigh, knocking it to the side and off of Angie.

Park's gun rang out. The corpse flew back a few feet and landed on its back, head destroyed.

Angie stood and glared at Mr. Paulson. She looked at the fire. It was spreading badly.

"Okay, now let's go!" yelled Park.

"Not yet," said Angie. She moved to a wall next to the washing machines. "I hate to admit it, but Mr. Paulson's right." She pulled a fire extinguisher from the wall and moved to the fire. She pulled the pin and emptied the extinguisher into the flames. In a few seconds the flames died down and stopped.

"We don't want the place burning down before we get out," she said, moving to drop the extinguisher. The dried corpse of the woman, the one with the scalpel buried in her eye socket, stirred. She moaned and began to sit up.

"Shit," said Angie. She stepped over to where the corpse was struggling to right itself. She hoisted the extinguisher over her shoulders and threw it down at the corpse's head. The head imploded, sending dried skin and dust flying. The corpse fell down again and stopped moving.

Angie looked back at the others. She undid her belt and removed a jug of alcohol. She tied the belt back and took out Park's lighter.

"Now we can go."

Twenty-Four

Maylee slammed on the brakes. The car jerked forward, then rocked back. Dalton yelped and tugged at the seat belt dug into his shoulder.

"Damn it, your driving sucks, Maylee," he said.

"Be quiet," said Maylee. She was gripping the steering wheel and looking out at the junction they'd just come to. She hated that she had to move the seat so close to reach the pedals. "Which way to the good bridge?" she said.

"What?"

"You remember. The bridge. The new one."

Maylee looked both directions. There used to be one quick way to Mom's work from here. An old wooden bridge that tourists would come to look at in the summer. Then one year someone from the government pronounced it unsafe, put a landmark sign on it, and the state had to build a new one. The new bridge was built farther up the same road, crossing the river at a different point. Maylee had ridden to work with Mom dozens of times, first over one bridge, then the other. Now, in the dark and terror and the newness of driving herself, Maylee couldn't remember.

She turned to Dalton. "The one we won't fall off of and die."

Dalton looked up and down the road. "How should I know? Mom's the one who drives."

Maylee sighed and looked again. She looked in the rearview mirror and saw a corpse stumbling up to the car, far away still but visible in the red of her taillights. Time was up. She'd have to choose.

"Well damn it, I think it's this way," Maylee said, then turned right.

For several minutes they drove in quiet. Trees went by in the dark, and every so often Maylee was sure she saw a corpse wandering among them. Then the bridge came into view. It was the new one. Maylee sighed with relief.

Then they drew closer and she noticed the corpses wandering up and down the bridge. Easily a hundred of them. Maybe more. Where had they all come from?

Maylee noticed their highly decomposed state and their tattered clothes. *The old graveyard nearby. This town's full of old graveyards.*

Maylee stopped the car and cursed.

"What?" said Dalton, then he looked out the window. "Oh."

"Maybe we can just run over them," said Maylee. She drummed her fingers on the steering wheel, wondering. There were more of them than she had run over in the garage. Lots more.

"You sure?" asked Dalton.

"No of course I'm not sure," said Maylee. "But it's that, the old rickety bridge, or going all the way back and taking the long way around."

"That would take forever," said Dalton.

"That's why we're doing this," said Maylee. She gunned the engine and tore for the bridge.

The nearest corpse turned just as Maylee smacked into it. It flew backward a few feet into the mass of corpses behind it. The car slowed to a stop. The corpses groaned and clawed at the car.

"Crap!" said Dalton. "Try harder!"

Maylee did. She floored the gas and the wheels spun as they had in the garage. The corpses hissed, their sheer mass keeping the car from moving more than a few feet at a time. One corpse, an old man in a rotted priest's collar, climbed up onto the hood. He scraped yellow fingernails across the windshield, trying to get at Maylee.

"Screw this," said Maylee. "We'll back up and try again."

She put the car in reverse and looked behind her. Her chest went tight. The corpses had surrounded the car.

"Shit," she said, still looking.

"What?" asked Dalton, turning to look. He gasped and was silent.

The priest on the hood groaned and pawed at the windshield. Another corpse, a woman in a torn and dirty dress, climbed onto the trunk. She gurgled and tried to bite through the glass.

"Go! Go!" yelled Dalton.

Maylee kept the car in reverse and slammed down on the gas. The car lurched backward, moving a few feet. More corpses appeared in back of the car. Maylee cursed and slammed on the gas again. Something under the car went "crunch" and the car was free. It moved faster than Maylee had anticipated and she swerved backward into the guardrail. The corpse on the trunk flew off. The corpse on the hood slammed into the windshield, cracking it slightly.

"Damn it!" yelled Maylee, wrenching the car into drive. She gave the car gas but it stayed in place. The guardrail creaked and groaned. The corpses began surrounding the car again. The priest on the hood ran his withered hands over the cracked windshield.

"Maylee..." said Dalton, his voice shaking as he stared at the priest.

"I'm working on it," said Maylee, pushing the gearshift into reverse and slamming the gas pedal. The car rocked backward. The guardrail creaked. The priest on the hood bit at the glass, his thick drool running down onto the hood.

"Maylee.."

"I said I'm working on it!" Maylee shifted into drive and gave the car gas. The engine roared but the car wouldn't move. She could hear the guardrail straining and groaning.

"Oh crap, Maylee!" said Dalton, a new urgency in his voice.

Maylee looked up. A new wave of corpses were stumbling onto the bridge. Nearly a hundred of them. They all looked torn and dirty. Some of them barely looked human, more like dried husks. Their skin cracked and split as they moved.

"Where are they coming from?" said Dalton.

The priest on the hood pounded on the windshield.

Maylee nodded at a steeple among the trees on the far side of the bridge.

"See that old church?"

"The church?" said Dalton. "These things come from churches?"

"No, Dalton," said Maylee, pulling the car into reverse and gunning the gas. The car stayed put. "The graveyard behind the church." She put the car into drive and tried again. Nothing. "Who knows how many more there are. We've got to get out of here."

"No crap," said Dalton.

The priest on the hood moaned and drooled. The corpses ahead of the car, now growing in numbers, pressed forward. Maylee looked in the rearview mirror. Another corpse, a man with a large portion of his face burnt and blackened, was pawing at the trunk.

Maylee shifted into park and took her foot off the gas.

"What the crap are you doing?" said Dalton.

Maylee reached into the backseat and grabbed the bat. "Stay here."

She opened the door. The smell of the corpses flooded in.

"Maylee!" yelled Dalton.

"Just stay here!" she said, undoing her seat belt and climbing from the car.

She had little room to move. The car was up against the guardrail. She slid her way clear of the door and shut it. The corpses were everywhere, groaning and reaching at her. The car kept them at bay. For the moment.

She gripped the bat and sidestepped to the back of the car. The burnt-face man groaned at her.

"Fuck off," she said, slamming the bat across his head. His head rocked to one side and a chunk of burnt flesh flew off and onto the road behind the car. He fell onto his back, groaning and pawing at nothing.

Maylee looked down where the car met the guardrail. The bumper had somehow hooked itself onto the metal of the rail. She frowned and whacked the bumper with the bat. The metal bent inward but was still hung on the rail.

The burnt-face man stood up. His newly-exposed flesh was red and raw. He growled at her, reaching.

"I said fuck off!" said Maylee, slamming his head again. He groaned and fell back down.

Maylee whacked the bumper again. The metal crumpled and came free of the rail.

"Damn right," she said to no one. She turned and looked around. The corpses from the graveyard were close to the car. The priest on the hood was doing his best to climb onto the car's roof. He was reaching for her desperately, clutching at air.

She sidestepped, quickly as she could, back to the door. She opened the door and slid back in, tossing the bat into the backseat.

"What the crap!" said Dalton.

"Not now," said Maylee, closing the door. She pulled the car into reverse and turned the wheel hard to the right. She gunned the gas and the car lurched free of the guardrail and into the middle of the bridge. She heard crunching and squishing and knew they were corpses.

The priest on the hood groaned and slid off the car, smacking his head on the windshield on his way down. The glass cracked a little more.

"Go go go!" said Dalton.

Maylee straightened the wheel and gunned the engine. The car sped backward, bouncing as it hit the road and was free of the bridge. For a panicked moment Maylee lost control of the car as it rocketed backward.

"Shit!" she said, slamming on the brakes. The car spun in the road and they both screamed.

The car came to a halt longways across the road. The back tires were very close to a ditch.

"Dammit!" said Dalton. "Your driving sucks, Maylee!"

Maylee ignored him and looked over at the bridge. It was now choked so thick with corpses there was no way they'd get across it.

"Shut up," she finally said, pulling the shifter into drive and turning the car to face away from the bridge. She took one last look at the bridge, then sped away.

"Looks like we have to try the old bridge," she said.

Twenty-Five

Angie walked down the hall as quietly as she could. Park was behind her doing the same. Kristen and Mr. Paulson were behind Park. Kristen looked up and down the hall, saying nothing. Mr. Paulson had his chair on the lowest setting, moving slowly and quietly.

Angie slowed to a halt as they approached a doorway to their right. The doorway to the hospital chapel. It was open and Angie could hear groaning. She held up a hand and the others stopped.

"Fuck," whispered Park. "More?"

Angie leaned forward and looked into the chapel. A group of corpses knelt near the altar. They were facing to one side, chewing on something on the floor. Angie saw bare legs and the bottom of a hospital robe. The rest was hidden behind a pew. Blood covered the bare legs.

"Yeah," whispered Angie. "More."

"Shit on this," whispered Mr. Paulson. "Just shoot them and let's go."

"We've been over this, dick-neck," whispered Park. "We don't have enough ammo for that."

"They're looking the other way and they haven't heard us," whispered Angie. "Let's just get past them and go. The cafeteria's just up ahead."

"Oh good," whispered Mr. Paulson. "I was hoping for some more of your fuck-awful food"

"Now, Dad," whispered Kristen. Her voice, even in a whisper, sounded hollow.

Angie said nothing, looking back into the chapel. The corpses still had not noticed them. She nodded to the others and they moved forward. They slowly and quietly crept past the doorway. The only sounds were the groaning of the feeding corpses and the soft whir of Mr. Paulson's chair.

A few steps later and they were clear of the room. Angie relaxed a little but stayed slow and quiet. They all made their way farther down the hall.

Eventually, the hallway opened into the cafeteria. Two rows of long tables ran along the center of the room, with several chairs at each one. At the far end of the room was another door, opening back into the hallway.

"Okay," said Angie, stepping over to the nearest table. "We can take a second to regroup." She set down the half-empty alcohol jug and undid the belt holding the remaining full ones to her waist.

She looked over at Park. He was taking his rifle off of his shoulder and looking around. She stepped over to him and spoke softly. "What did you mean earlier?"

He frowned at her. "What?"

"You said something about getting your wish if we ran out of ammo and died."

He looked around and rubbed his stubble. "You heard that?"

"Yeah," said Angie. "And we don't need that kind of..."

"Look, I didn't really mean you. Or them. I meant me."

Angie frowned.

"Listen," said Park, quietly. "Before we came here, before I brought Moe to the hospital I mean, I was planning on killing myself."

Angie blinked.

Park nodded. "Probably would have used this very same fucking rifle to do it, too." He shook the rifle in his hand and set it down on a nearby table.

"Why didn't you?"

Park shrugged. "Got distracted."

Angie looked down at the floor and chuckled. "You know, before tonight I would have asked you why anyone would want to do such a thing. Now I almost have a hard time understanding why someone wouldn't."

Park smirked at her and she smirked back.

"So why do you keep going?" she asked.

"I honestly don't know."

Park dug a box of ammo from his hunting jacket. He gave the box a little shake and cursed. "I'm damned near out."

"Same here," said Kristen, following Mr. Paulson as he wheeled his chair over to where Angie had set the jugs of alcohol.

"We'll just have to be smart," said Angie, stepping over to Mr. Paulson.

"Can't be something you're not, honey," muttered Mr. Paulson.

"Dad," said Kristen, quietly. "Hush."

Mr. Paulson whirled the chair around to face Kristen. "Stop telling me to hush! Have you stopped for a second to consider how roundly fucked we all are? We've got the hillbilly, the maid, the cripple and you. And what the fuck have you ever been good for? You couldn't even put your goddamned husband out of his goddamned misery!"

Kristen took a step back, her mouth open. Her eyes were wet.

Angie slammed the jug of alcohol down. "Keep it down. They will hear us."

"You shut the fuck up too!" Mr. Paulson roared. "You stomping around like you're somehow in fucking charge! You could barely manage my fucking bed pan as it was! You're so fucking stupid I'm surprised your kids haven't been taken away already!"

Angie circled the wheelchair to face him, not sure what she would do but sure it would be bad. She stopped when she heard groans coming from both doorways.

"Great," she said. "Good job."

Corpses staggered into the door at the far end of the room. The corpse at the front, a woman in a bloody dress, hissed and lurched at them.

"Shit!" said Park, leveling his rifle at the woman and firing. The woman's head snapped back and she crumpled. "We don't have enough ammo for this!"

Groans came from behind them. Angie spun to see more corpses stumble through the door at their backs. A man with no pants was chewing on one of the bloody legs Angie had seen in the chapel. He bit free a red chunk from the top of the leg and chewed.

Angie spun back to face Mr. Paulson. He was quiet, looking back and forth from one group of corpses to the other. "Any ideas?" she said.

Mr. Paulson said nothing, looking back and forth.

"I said any ideas!" she shrieked at him. The approaching corpses groaned from both sides. She felt her sanity slipping.

"He's just an old man!" yelled Kristen, wiping tears from her cheeks.

Angie turned to Kristen, her hand raised to smack her. She stopped, saying nothing.

"Remember that part when I said we were running out of ammo?" said Park, turning to face the other way and shooting the leg-carrying corpse. The corpse dropped the leg and fell.

Angie turned and grabbed the edge of the table nearest to her. "Here," she said. "Push the tables together." She shoved the table up against the next table in the row. "It'll buy us some time."

Park nodded and slung the rifle over his shoulder. He grabbed chairs away from the tables and tossed them aside. He and Angie pushed two more of the tables together.

Kristen was just standing there, staring at the approaching corpses.

"Get your ass over here!" yelled Park.

Kristen glared at him but rushed over. After a few seconds of pushing and tugging, they had put four of the long tables together, creating a raised platform.

"Everyone up!" yelled Angie.

Park jumped up onto the platform and grabbed Kristen's arms.

"But Dad!" she said, pulling back.

"But your ass!" said Park, grabbing her arms tighter and wrenching her up onto the platform.

Mr. Paulson wheeled himself over to the side of the platform. Corpses were closing in on him from both sides. "What the fuck?"

Angie hopped up onto the platform. The corpses coming from behind reached the tables. They reached for Park and Kristen, but the platform was too wide. One corpse, a fresher-looking one, began climbing onto the platform. Park kicked him off. The others were too rotted or too wounded to quickly climb.

Angie stepped over to Mr. Paulson and looked down. The corpses were getting closer.

"What the fuck! You lousy bitch!" He screamed up at her.

"Dad!" Kristen said, rushing toward the edge of the table. Angie pushed her back, so hard Kristen almost fell off the other side and into the waiting arms of the corpses. Angie looked down at Mr. Paulson.

"*I said any ideas!*" she shrieked down at him.

"No!" said Mr. Paulson. The corpses were getting very close now. "No, goddammit, no!"

"Park," said Angie, "help me."

She knelt and grabbed Mr. Paulson's arm. Park came over and grabbed the other one. They wrenched Mr. Paulson up onto the platform. He landed in the center of the tables, unable to stand.

"You be more careful with him!" yelled Kristen, leveling her gun at Park.

Angie looked down at Mr. Paulson. "I am sorry. But never say anything like that to me again. Me or your daughter."

Mr. Paulson glared up at her but said nothing.

Park kicked at another corpse that was beginning to crawl up onto the platform. "We don't have enough bullets for all of these!"

A corpse grabbed Mr. Paulson's legs. He screamed as the corpse dragged him toward its open mouth.

"Dad!" yelled Kristen, moving her rifle toward the corpse. She fired just as the corpse leaned in to bite. The bullet caught the corpse in the temple. The corpse grunted, then slid off Mr. Paulson and onto the floor.

"Goddammit!" yelled Mr. Paulson. "This is it, assholes! We're dead!"

Another corpse grabbed Mr. Paulson from behind. He screamed. Park was busy kicking at another corpse. Kristen spun and pulled the trigger on her rifle. Nothing happened. "Oh god!" she said. "I'm out!"

The corpse that had hold of Mr. Paulson pulled itself further up onto the platform. It moaned ecstatically and pulled Mr. Paulson toward its mouth.

"Shit!" said Angie. She reached above her and pushed at the panel covering the florescent lights. She pulled the panel free and tossed it aside. Mr. Paulson was struggling with the corpse.

Angie pulled free her belt, letting the jugs of alcohol tumble to the platform. She wrapped the belt around her hand and grabbed hold of one of the florescent tubes above her. She wrenched it free and slammed it into the head of the corpse that had hold of Mr. Paulson. The glass tube shattered and the corpse faltered, letting go. Angie screamed and shoved the broken end of the tube into the corpse's face. It stuck and held. She kicked the tube and knocked the corpse to the floor.

"How many shots you got left?" she asked Park.

"Not nearly enough," he said, reloading the rifle.

She nodded and picked up one of the alcohol jugs. She turned to Kristen. "Give me your scalpel!"

Kristen said nothing, getting the scalpel from her pocket and giving it to Angie.

"What are you doing?" said Park, cocking the rifle.

"Watch," said Angie. She held up the plastic jug and stabbed it with the scalpel several times in several different spots. Alcohol began leaking out of the slits.

"What the hell..." said Mr. Paulson.

"Shoot!" Angie yelled, flinging the jug into the air toward the exit door. Alcohol spilled out of the jug as it flew. Park followed the jug with his rifle and fired just as it was suspended over the bulk of the corpses blocking their way. The jug exploded into a fireball and fell on the corpses below. The corpses groaned more loudly and started scattering across the room. Flaming corpses hit other corpses, setting them alight.

"I thought they don't feel pain," said Kristen.

"They don't," said Park. "But they're afraid of fire!"

In a few more seconds, the corpses had scattered enough to clear a path to the door.

"Get Mr. Paulson!" said Angie, kneeling to get the last two full jugs of alcohol. She ran to the edge of the platform and leapt off.

Park slung his rifle over his shoulder and stepped up to Mr. Paulson. He knelt and lifted him up off the platform.

"Put me down!" yelled Mr. Paulson. "I'm not a child!"

"Be careful with him!" yelled Kristen.

Angie ran to the wheelchair. The flaming corpses were stumbling around and groaning. Angie grabbed the chair's controller and wheeled it around to the front of the platform. One of the flaming corpses, more decayed than the others, fell over and was still.

"Huh," said Park. "Fire does kill them eventually." Then he hopped off the table, Mr. Paulson in his arms.

"Shit!" said Mr. Paulson as Park landed. "Be careful."

Park said nothing, putting Mr. Paulson back in his seat. Mr. Paulson glared at everyone, adjusting his robe and grabbing hold of the controller.

Angie looked around the room. The flaming corpses were spreading the fire fast. Soon the room itself would be ablaze.

Kristen jumped off the platform. "Are you okay, Dad?"

"All of you fuck off!" said Mr. Paulson.

"We gotta go," said Angie, leading them to the exit door and back to the hallway.

Twenty-Six

Maylee drove as fast as she dared through the dark. Trees appeared and disappeared in the headlights.

"Slow down," said Dalton.

"Can't," she said. "We gotta get there. We gotta help Mom."

The road they were on was empty. No cars and few houses. They were almost outside of town now, running along the back-road shortcut Mom had taken to work before the old bridge closed. If they could get across the old wooden bridge, then it would be a short run down another back road to the hospital.

Maylee knew she was driving too fast. She couldn't help it. Her chest was pounding from the first bridge. *I almost got us both killed*, she kept thinking.

She could hear Dalton squirming in his seat next to her. She could *sense* it. She knew she should slow down.

"Can't," she muttered again, mostly to herself. "We gotta help Mom."

She rounded a bend and suddenly the bridge was there.

Both she and Dalton gasped and she slammed on the brakes.

The tires screeched and the car slid from side to side but eventually stopped a few feet from the bridge. Dalton was leaning as far forward as his locked seat belt would allow. He sat back and rubbed his shoulder. "Ow, Maylee!"

"Shhh," said Maylee, looking out at the bridge. A chain was tied from one post to another, blocking the way. A sign hung on the chain. In the headlights, Maylee could see that it read *Unsafe, do not use. Future site of historical marker.*

"Crap," said Dalton, looking out the window. "How are we supposed to get across?"

"It's just a chain, Dalton," said Maylee, undoing her seat belt. "We're lucky. Mom says eventually there'll be a big concrete post blocking the way. And there'd be no way we could move that. But we should be able to move a chain."

Dalton undid his seat belt. "I'll help."

"No, you'll stay here."

"Come on, Maylee. I can do it. It looks clear out there, anyway."

Maylee looked out the front window and sighed. It did look clear.

She pressed the control switch and her window slid down with a whir The cool night air blew in with no stench of bodies. She listened.

It was quiet except for typical night noises. Insects chittered. Leaves and grass rustled in the occasional breeze. No screams. No moaning.

"It's fine," she said after a few moments, breathing out. "So okay. I guess you can come. Just hurry. Let's get the chain unhooked, then get across."

She opened the door, leaving the engine running. Stepping out, she took another look around. Everything still looked clear.

Dalton got out and shut his door. He rubbed his arms. "It's cold."

"Yeah," said Maylee. "Come on, let's hurry."

She stepped over to the bridge, Dalton following. The chain ran from one wooden guardrail post to the other. Maylee walked over to one post and looked. The chain was simply wrapped around it and hooked with a nail.

"Wow," said Dalton, looking with her. "Low budget."

"Told you," said Maylee, smiling in the dark. She nodded across the road to the other post. "Go unhook that one."

Dalton nodded and trotted to the other side. Maylee grabbed the chain on her side and pulled it off the nail. She unwound the chain and looked over to Dalton. "Got it?"

"Got it," said Dalton, holding up his end of the chain.

A corpse grabbed Maylee from behind. Maylee gasped. She saw Dalton's eyes grow wide.

"Maylee!" he yelled, running toward her.

The corpse behind her groaned and pulled her into the woods. Maylee screamed and kicked, reaching back to push at the corpse's head. She felt slimy, cold skin and heard the corpse moaning and working its jaws. Maylee still gripped the chain and it dragged on the ground in front of her. She thrashed her head around, avoiding the thing's mouth.

The chain caught on a thick tree root. Maylee saw her chance and yanked herself forward, using the chain as leverage. She slipped from the corpse's grasp and fell to the ground. She spun around and looked up.

The corpse was an old man with a bloated belly and rotting skin. A portion of his throat was missing, and Maylee could see the cords in the man's neck moving up and down as he gnashed his teeth.

"Maylee!" yelled Dalton, careening out of the darkness. He screamed as he ran straight into the corpse.

The corpse groaned and wrapped its arms around Dalton.

Maylee clambered to her feet and looked around frantically for a weapon. Why had she left the bat in the car? The chain in her hand would have to do.

The corpse bent in to bite Dalton's throat. Maylee swung the chain over her head and whipped it at the corpse. The thick metal links caught the corpse in the cheek. It grunted and stepped back, letting go of Dalton. Dalton screamed and ran over to Maylee.

Maylee was mad now. She swung the chain again at the corpse, this time harder. The corpse grabbed at them and the chain whacked off two rotten fingers.

"Maylee, come on!" said Dalton, pulling her back toward the car.

"Not yet," she said. She twirled the chain round and round over her head. She gave it as much slack as the tree root behind her would allow. The corpse reached for her. She grunted and whipped the chain forward.

The chain wrapped tightly around the corpse's arm. The corpse kept moving toward her, oblivious to the chain.

"Shit," she said. "Okay, let's go."

They both turned and ran through the trees toward the headlights of the car. She could hear the corpse groaning behind her. It sounded further and further away.

Dalton, ahead of her, reached the road and ran for the car. Maylee reached the road and turned around. The corpse was still far behind them. It was tugging at the chain, which was still wrapped around its arm and caught on the root.

She smiled and flipped off the corpse. Then turned and ran back to the car.

Dalton was already inside and shutting the passenger door. "Come on!"

Maylee flopped into the driver's seat and slammed her door. Her window was still down and she could hear the corpse groaning and the chain rattling.

She put the car into drive and started forward.

As soon as they hit the bridge she heard loud groaning and cracking. She stopped.

"Shit," she said.

"Was that the bridge?" said Dalton, looking around.

"Yeah," said Maylee, swallowing. "Yeah it was."

Wood cracked underneath them. She heard something hit the river below with a splash.

"Crap, Maylee," said Dalton. "Let's go back."

Maylee shook her head. "No, we've lost too much time as it is. We have to get to Mom."

She eased the car forward. The bridge creaked and shook, but held.

She eased the car to a stop and looked at Dalton. "There, see? We'll just go slow and..."

With a groan, the bloated old man appeared just outside Maylee's window. His arm was missing.

Dalton screamed. The corpse reached its remaining arm into the car. Maylee fumbled with the window control, hitting the door handle instead. The door swung open, knocking into the corpse. The corpse's arm hooked around the door as it swung out.

The corpse slammed into the wooden guardrail. The rail snapped and fell away. The wood under the driver's side rear tire gave way and the car slumped to one side.

Both Maylee and Dalton screamed as the car leaned out over the river. The door dangled out over the water, the corpse hanging from it. The corpse groaned and bit up at Maylee.

More cracking came from underneath them. The car rocked. Dalton was still screaming.

Maylee turned in her seat and kicked down at the corpse's head. It bit at her shoes as she slammed the soles into the corpse's face. She grunted and kicked down as hard as she could.

With a horrible tearing sound the corpse's torso came free of its remaining arm. Still biting up at Maylee, the armless corpse fell to the river below and vanished with a splash.

The car shook as more wood fell from the bridge. Maylee reached out over the water - willing herself not to look down - and grabbed the door handle. She slammed the door shut. The corpse's arm snapped as the door closed on it. The remains of the arm bounced off the bridge and down into the water.

"Hurry!" said Dalton. Maylee heard more cracking and groaning. Wood was falling into the water so fast there were almost no breaks in the sound.

Maylee slammed on the gas and the car raced forward. The car bounced as wood fell away underneath it.

The headlights lit up the chain across the other end of the bridge. They both screamed. Then Maylee squared her jaw. There was no other choice. She gunned the engine more and the car picked up speed.

The car hit the chain and Maylee's heart leapt when it snapped. The car reached pavement just as a huge chunk of the bridge fell away into the river. Maylee screeched to a halt. The second chain and sign flew away from the front of the car, clattering to the road.

Both Maylee and Dalton looked over their shoulders. The bridge gave a final groan and collapsed into the river.

"We're in so much trouble," said Dalton.

"I think the world has more things to worry about right now," said Maylee. She turned back and gave the car gas.

Twenty-Seven

The cafeteria was in flames behind them as Angie and Park rushed down the hallway. Kristen and Mr. Paulson followed.

"Shit," said Angie, stopping and turning back to look. "We really have to hurry now. No way we're putting that out."

Alarms went off all over the hospital. A splitting, piercing ringing.

"And this is when the sprinklers would be going off?" said Park, looking around.

"Yeah," said Angie. "Come on." She turned to look back at the others. Kristen was walking toward her.

"What?" said Angie just as Kristen balled up her fist and punched her.

"Don't you ever fucking treat my father that way!" she screamed.

Angie dropped the jugs of alcohol she was carrying. She flashed red and shoved Kristen away. "Back off, bitch! You want to beat my ass, wait 'til we get fucking outside!"

"Hey!" yelled Park. "As much as I love a good cat fight, we really *really* need to fucking get!"

Kristen glared at Angie. She rushed her, slamming her into the wall and grabbing her hair. Angie screamed and rammed her knee into Kristen's stomach.

* * *

"Come the fuck on!" said Park, yelling at Angie and Kristen. Mr. Paulson watched as his daughter and Angie fought in the hallway. He could feel the heat from the cafeteria behind them, even though it was a good twenty feet.

He said nothing, looking at Kristen's pale face. He knew the look. She was spent. It was the same look she had when she'd spent all day caring for him. The same look she had when Sam would go off by himself and do whatever the fuck it was he used to do.

He looked at Angie as she struggled with Kristen. The bitch had almost got him killed. Maybe he was asking for it. Maybe he *wanted* it. He should have died years ago. Did people think he liked being a tired old man who couldn't even fucking stand up anymore? Did people think he liked sucking away at his daughter's time? He could barely get to the toilet himself anymore. How long before he had to wear a goddamned diaper and lay on the bed while his *daughter* changed him?

He heard groaning come from the cafeteria. He wheeled himself around to look. Down the hallway corpses were approaching through the flames.

He turned back to the others. They were arguing with each other.

He started to say something, then shut his mouth. Fuck it. Fuck *this*.

He looked one last time at Kristen. *I'm sorry*, he thought.

He wheeled the chair around to face back toward the cafeteria. He pushed the controller forward and moved toward the door. The corpses were just starting to emerge.

"Here I come, fuckers," he said. With his free hand, he reached behind himself and pulled the tube from his oxygen tank. He heard the slight hiss of the nozzle next to his ear.

The corpses saw him coming and groaned in welcome. Mr. Paulson reached over his head and twisted the regulator open as far as it would go. The oxygen blasted him in the back of the head, the hiss of it almost drowning out the groaning of the corpses.

"Dad?" came Kristen's voice far behind him.

I'm sorry.

The corpses closed in on him. He fished out his lighter, held it up to the oxygen nozzle, and lit it.

* * *

The explosion shook the hallway.

"Dad!" screamed Kristen, rushing toward the fireball.

"No!" Angie grabbed Kristen and pulled her back.

"Let me fucking go!" Kristen screeched, struggling with Angie.

Flames leapt across the ceiling and walls. Corpses groaned. Kristen fell to her knees, sobbing. "Dad!"

Angie looked up ahead and her eyes grew wide. "Everybody down!"

She and Park dropped to the floor. Angie pushed Kristen over to lay flat. "Let me go!" Kristen yelled.

Mr. Paulson's wheelchair flew over their heads, slamming into the wall to their right. Flames from it coated the wall and shot up over their heads.

"Come on!" yelled Park, climbing to his feet.

"No!" yelled Kristen, reaching toward the cafeteria. All Angie could see up there were flames and the outline of corpses. "Dad!"

Angie grabbed Kristen's shoulders and pulled her to her feet. "Come on!"

"Dad!"

Angie turned Kristen around and pushed her forward, down the hallway. She bent to get the jugs of alcohol. One was too close to the flames. She grabbed the one she could safely get and stood.

"Come on!" she yelled.

She and Park ran down the hallway, Angie dragging Kristen with them.

Twenty-Eight

Maylee guided the car through another bend in the road. It was a little easier than before. She was getting the hang of this. She smiled to herself. *See, I'm not a kid anymore.*

Dalton was looking out his side window, watching trees speed by. He turned to her. "How much longer?"

"Not long at all," said Maylee.

Dalton nodded. "Okay, I'll get the bat so we won't forget it this time." He crawled around in his seat, reaching into the back.

Maylee shot a quick look over at him, then back at the road. "Hey, your seat belt isn't on!"

"So?"

"Put it on right now!" Maylee turned the wheel, going through another bend.

"I'm just getting the bat!"

"Dammit, Dalton!" she said. She took one hand off the wheel and pushed him back into his seat. "Put it on!"

He glared at her, then started to reach for the back seat again.

"Now!" Maylee yelled, doing her best Mom impression. Dalton sat back in his seat, looked at Maylee, then reached for his seat belt. He put it on and stuck his tongue out at her.

Maylee smiled and went around another corner.

Three corpses stood in the middle of the road.

Maylee and Dalton screamed as the headlights washed over the corpses. Maylee panicked and wrenched the wheel as far to the right as she could. The car screeched, slid down the road sideways, and flipped over.

For a moment all Maylee knew was the sound of crunching metal and breaking glass. And Dalton screaming.

Then her senses were too numb to know anything.

Then, slowly, they came back. She was upside down in her seat, hanging from the seat belt. Dalton coughed next to her.

Oh god, she thought, looking upside-down at the glass strewn across the road and smelling the burnt rubber of the tires. *I am just a kid. What the hell am I doing?*

She heard the sounds of feet shuffling to her right. The corpses were coming.

"Dalton?" she said. "Are you okay?"

"I think so."

Maylee fumbled with her seat belt. It detached and she fell to the top of the car. Her head banged against the ceiling. It smarted but she did her best to ignore it. The corpses were getting closer. She could hear them.

She got up to her knees and reached across Dalton to his seat belt. He seemed to be okay.

"Told you to wear this," she said, quietly.

She undid the latch and caught Dalton as he slid out of his seat.

A pair of legs appeared just outside the broken windshield.

"Shit," she said, easing Dalton down. "We gotta get out of here."

Moaning came from over the car. With a "pop" and the sound of flesh tearing, the corpse dropped to its knees. It was a woman in a flower-print dress. She moaned through cracked lips and reached for them.

Maylee turned to her window just in time to see another corpse crawling toward it. It was a man covered in scrapes and cuts. He reached out, clawing at her.

Dalton screamed from behind her. Maylee turned to see that the woman almost had him. She looked past Dalton to see his window was still shut. The car was too wrecked to even think about trying to get it open.

"Back seat!" she yelled, pulling him into the back and clear of the reaching corpses.

The woman at the front of the car climbed into the car after them. Her dress caught on a piece of glass, slowing her down. The woman grunted and tugged, reaching for Maylee and Dalton.

Dalton picked up the bat and swung it at the woman's hands. Maylee kicked at the back window. The window cracked but didn't give.

The corpse at the side window stuck its head inside. It bit and hissed at Dalton. Dalton swung the bat into the corpse's face, then back at the reaching woman. "Hurry!" he yelled.

Maylee kicked the back window a second time. Cracks spread through the glass but the window held.

The corpses up front and to the side reached back at them. Dalton furiously swung the bat from side to side.

"Dammit!" Maylee yelled, kicking the back window with all her might. The window gave. The window shattered outward.

Maylee pulled her leg back and turned to tug Dalton toward her. "Come on!"

They both crawled for the opening in the glass. *Wait*, Maylee thought as they crawled, *weren't there three corpses in the road?*

A rotten arm reached down from above and into the broken window. It caught Dalton by the hair and he screamed. Maylee could hear the corpse groaning from atop the overturned car.

Dalton pulled free and smacked the hand with the bat, nearly hitting Maylee in the head in the process.

"Watch it!" said Maylee.

The woman from behind them groaned and Maylee heard glass break. They looked back and saw that she was free of the glass. She was crawling into the car.

"Shit!" Maylee turned back to the grasping hand. She grabbed hold of it and pulled it toward her as hard as she could. The arm caught on the glass of the broken back window. Maylee tugged harder and the skin of the rotten arm tore and snapped. She fell back, the arm in her lap. She flung the arm aside and grabbed Dalton.

"Now!" she yelled, pulling him with her. They crawled out of the car, avoiding the rotten stump where the arm had been.

Out on the street, they stood and looked around. The car was in ruin. A corpse was atop the car, hissing at them. It had no arms. Apparently Maylee had broken off its last one.

"Serves you right!" she said.

"What?" said Dalton, looking around.

"Nothing," said Maylee, taking the bat from Dalton. She slammed it down on the corpse's head. The rotten head collapsed and the corpse fell forward, still. The other two corpses were crawling around in the car.

"Now what?" said Dalton.

Maylee looked around. She pointed the bat toward the woods. "The hospital should be just over the hill that way. If we take a shortcut through the woods, we should still get there pretty fast."

Dalton looked at the woods, then back at Maylee. After a few seconds, he nodded.

Maylee frowned down at him. "Are you scared?"

"No!" he glared at her.

"Well I am," she said. "But let's go anyway."

And with that they turned and ran into the woods.

Twenty-Nine

Angie raced down the hallway, Park and Kristen behind her. The fire alarm kept up its shrill clanging, all throughout the hospital. Smoke was coming from the hallway behind them.

"How much further?" said Park from behind.

"Not much," said Angie. "Just around the corner is the..." And she stopped.

Park and Kristen drew to a halt behind her. "What?" said Park.

Angie stepped around the corner. "The maternity ward."

Park and Kristen came up beside her.

A small room stood just to Angie's right. She stepped inside.

"I forgot," she said, cold dread creeping over her. "I can't believe I forgot."

A group of white hospital cribs stood in the room. The three closest ones rocked slowly from side to side.

Park and Kristen stepped in after her. "Forgot what?" said Kristen, her voice raw and thick.

Angie stepped over to the cribs and looked down. "The Wilson triplets."

In the cribs lay three identical infants. All three were gray with clouded eyes. They worked their toothless mouths open and closed. They fumbled at the air around them.

And Angie couldn't hear it over the loud and constant fire alarm, but she could tell they were moaning.

"Shit," said Park, looking down over Angie's shoulder.

"Oh god," said Kristen, stepping back. She put her hand over her mouth. "Oh god," she said again, muffled by her hand.

"How'd they die to begin with?" said Park.

"Who knows," said Angie. "They've been alone in here most of the night. Could have been anything."

"Oh god oh god oh god," Kristen kept repeating into her hand.

"Fuck if that ain't awful," said Park quietly.

They both looked at the babies in silence. Smoke built up in the hall outside and the fire alarm blared.

"Come on," said Park. "Let's go."

"No," said Angie, shaking her head. "I can't leave them like this."

Park looked at her. "They're already dead..."

Angie snapped her gaze to Park. "Do you have any children, Parker?"

Park looked at her for several seconds. The alarm blared and Kristen sobbed into her hand. "Yeah," he said finally. "Yeah I do. Haven't seem them for a long time, but yeah."

"Could you leave them in this state?"

Park looked at the cribs, then back at Angie. He nodded and took the rifle off his shoulder.

Angie shook her head. She felt like crying but pushed the tears back. "No. We're almost out of bullets, right?"

Park frowned and re-shouldered the gun. "Yeah. Just what do you have in mind?"

Angie swallowed and popped the lid off the remaining jug of alcohol.

"Oh god!" said Kristen from behind them.

Angie looked at Park and bit her lip. He looked at her and sighed. "Better than just leaving them like this."

Angie nodded and turned back to the cribs. The babies thrashed around and kicked their gray legs. They blinked their clouded eyes.

"I'm so sorry," she whispered down to them.

Then she poured the alcohol across all three cribs. The babies showed no reaction to the splashing liquid.

She took out Park's lighter. "We are sure they don't feel pain, right?"

"Pretty sure," said Park.

Angie took a breath and flicked the lighter on.

"Oh god oh god oh god," said Kristen.

Angie held the flame to the edge of the sheet hanging out of each crib. Flames quickly engulfed all three. The babies showed no reaction. They continued to move around slowly, chewing with their toothless mouths at nothing.

A few moments later the babies were still.

Then they were lost in flames.

Angie turned to Park and Kristen. Park's face was blank. Kristen was looking at her with wide, accusing eyes.

"Let's go," said Angie, dropping the empty jug and moving for the door.

Thirty

The woods were darker than Maylee had anticipated. The headlights of the wrecked car were far behind them now and the moon did little good through the thick covering of trees. It was fall, but not enough leaves had fallen to allow much light.

"It's dark," said Dalton, gripping Maylee's hand. It had taken a lot for him to agree to hold it.

"I know," said Maylee, stepping over a root and guiding Dalton around a tree. "That's why we have to stay close to each other. If we keep walking forward we should get to the road again soon. Right across from the hospital."

Was she sure about that? She wondered. It was very dark and they could have so easily gotten turned around among all the trees. At least it was quiet. No corpses could be heard groaning.

Of course, in this dark it would only take one.

Maylee swallowed, tried not to think about that, and kept walking.

"How much further?" said Dalton after a few more steps.

"Don't know yet," said Maylee. "We're still going uphill, so a little ways yet."

"I can barely see anything." Dalton's hand was sweaty in hers.

"I know," said Maylee, looking around and gripping the bat with her other hand. "But once we get to the top of the hill, we should be able to see the lights from the hospital parking lot. That should help."

Dalton said nothing and they kept walking. After a few seconds, Dalton stopped.

"What?" said Maylee, stopping with him.

"I heard something."

Maylee fell quiet, listening. First she heard nothing. Then, a rustle.

"Maybe it's the wind," she whispered.

Then, a moan.

"Shit," she whispered hoarsely into the dark. "Down!"

She dropped to her knees. Dalton dropped down next to her.

They both listened intently. From their left they heard moaning and rustling. The sound of something moving through the underbrush.

"It's coming!" whispered Dalton.

"Shhh!" whispered Maylee. "We'll just let it pass, then keep going. It won't see or hear us down here."

Wouldn't it? She wondered. She *hoped*.

They lay in silence a few seconds longer. The rustling grew louder. Maylee braced, waiting for the sight of stumbling, rotten legs.

A rotten face appeared, inches from hers. It was a corpse missing both legs, dragging itself along on its elbows.

Maylee screamed. Dalton screamed.

The corpse hissed and reached for Maylee. It had a rotten, slimy face and it ground yellow teeth at her. The face was so decomposed Maylee couldn't tell what gender the thing was.

Maylee tried to jump up but the thing grabbed hold of her hair. Dalton leapt to his feet and started screaming. The corpse pulled, stronger than Maylee would have expected, and she slid across the grass and twigs toward the corpse's rotten mouth. Maylee swung the bat in her hand, but the angle would not let her connect with the corpse's head.

"The bat, Dalton!" she yelled, straining her head back away from the corpse's teeth. "Get the bat!"

She heard Dalton start to move. Then he was screaming. She heard a second corpse groaning.

"Maylee!" Dalton yelled. "There's another one!"

"Shit," Maylee muttered to herself. The corpse pulled harder and she slid closer to the mouth. Maylee dropped the bat, put her hands in the dirt and dug in her fingers. She clenched her knees and wrenched herself up. The corpse kept hold of her hair. Maylee rose up and the corpse rose with her. The corpse crashed into Maylee's chest and knocked her over backward.

Maylee landed on her back, the legless corpse on top of her. It groaned and bit at her. Maylee pushed the corpse up and away from her. The corpse kept hold of her hair. Maylee pushed as hard as she could. She felt her scalp strain as the corpse pulled and tugged.

Somewhere nearby, Dalton was screaming.

Maylee glanced to her left and saw a rotting log. A sharp broken branch jutted up from it. She put her foot up underneath her and shoved. She rolled, still holding the corpse, over to the log. They reached the log and Maylee rolled on top of it, the corpse under her.

She heard a thick "chunk" noise as the branch punctured the back of the corpse's head.

The corpse hissed and bit at her.

Maylee grunted and shoved the corpse's head farther down. The branch shot up through the corpse's eye and Maylee snapped her head up, avoiding the explosion of thick blood and muck. The corpse hissed once more and slumped.

Dalton screamed to Maylee's right.

Maylee stood and ran to Dalton. Dalton was struggling with a corpse, a fat woman with cuts and scrapes all over her body. He was pushing her back, keeping away from her mouth.

"Maylee!" he yelled.

"Hold on!" she screamed. She ran over to where she had dropped the bat and snatched it up, barely breaking her stride. She was back to Dalton and the corpse in seconds.

Screaming in fury, she swung the bat at the corpse. The bat barely missed the top of Dalton's head and slammed into the woman's face. She blinked and let go of Dalton. She groaned at Maylee and reached for her.

Maylee screamed again and slammed the bat down on the woman's head. A bloody split appeared in the woman's face and she staggered back. Maylee let out a feral roar and rammed the bat down again. The woman's head split and fell to either side. Brains and blood slid down the woman's front. The woman fell over still.

Maylee stood, panting down at the woman.

Dalton stepped over. "Maylee?"

She whipped her head over to him. "You okay?"

"Yeah."

"Good. Fuck this. We're running."

She grabbed his hand and started running up the hill. Within a few seconds they could see light coming from up ahead.

The hospital, Maylee thought. *Just over the hill and across the road.*

Almost there.

Thirty-One

Angie stepped away from the maternity ward, heading down the hall. Soon they would be just outside the emergency room. Then, outside. Hopefully in time for Maylee and Dalton.

"Hey, we gotta move," she heard Park say behind her.

She stopped and turned. Kristen was standing just outside the maternity ward, shaking her head and sobbing.

Angie stepped back over, sighing. "Come on, Kristen, we have to keep moving."

"No!" she spit, flashing red wet eyes at Angie. "I can't!"

Park sighed, looking back up the hallway. The smoke was getting thicker and the alarm kept ringing. Even with the alarm, Angie thought she heard groans approaching. "Look, sweetheart, we gotta..."

"You shut up!" Kristen yelled. "Both of you! You're both awful, awful people! Sam's dead, Dad's dead, and the whole fucking world is dead!"

Moaning corpses rounded the corner behind them.

Park saw them and grabbed Kristen's arm. He started to pull her down the hallway but she wrenched away.

"Let go of me!" she screamed, putting her hands to her head. "And someone shut off that goddamned ringing!"

"Kristen!" Angie yelled, hoping to snap her out of it. "Come on!"

Kristen looked at Angie with wide eyes. *Oh shit*, Angie thought. *She's gone.*

"The whole world is dead," Kristen said again, quietly.

Smoke billowed and the alarm clanged. The corpses drew near.

Kristen noticed the corpses and turned. "Oh look. Here comes the world now. All of it dead."

She stepped toward the corpses.

"Kristen, no!" yelled Angie, lunging forward.

Park grabbed for Kristen but she pulled away, spinning around to glare at them.

"*I said keep your hands off of me!*" she shrieked, backing away and into the waiting arms of a corpse.

"Sam?" she said, turning around.

But it wasn't Sam. It was a young man wearing a t-shirt with a beer logo. And with a huge rip in both the shirt and his chest underneath.

She screamed as the man bit into her neck.

"No!" yelled Angie.

Kristen bucked and jerked as her blood spewed out across the man's face. The man chewed and moaned. Several other corpse hands closed on Kristen, pushing her backward.

Her body bent over backward as more corpses bit into her arms and chest. Her head fell back and Angie could see her still blinking. Blood ran out of her mouth.

"The whole world..." Kristen said, rasping through the hole in her throat, "...is dead."

Park ran over to Angie. Angie couldn't stop staring. The corpses fed as the smoke billowed behind them. The alarm clanged all around.

"Come on!" said Park, tugging on her.

Angie stared.

"I said come the fuck on!"

Angie blinked at Park, then nodded her head.

They both turned and ran.

Thirty-Two

Angie and Park ran to the corner and stopped. Smoke was building up. The screeching alarm drowned out the sounds of corpses eating Kristen far behind them. The lights flickered.

Park looked around. "Fuck. Wonder how long we have until the power goes out completely?"

"There's a back-up generator," said Angie. "It should kick in about a minute after the power goes out."

Park nodded.

Angie braced herself and peeked around the corner. A few corpses were wandering just up ahead, their backs to Angie.

She ducked back. "Got a few up ahead. How many bullets you got left?"

"Not nearly enough."

Angie nodded, then gasped as one of the corpses grabbed her throat from around the corner.

"Shit!" yelled Park. He pointed the rifle right next to her ear and fired.

There was an explosion of sound, then silence. Then a ringing. A high-pitched whine. She felt Park grab her and pull her away from the corner. As she spun, she saw the corpse that had grabbed her. Part of its head was exploded away. It was sliding down the wall, still. The other corpses were coming around the corner.

She heard Park yelling something, his voice muffled and buried under the ringing. Then she could hear muffled moans and the sound of the fire alarm.

Park jerked her backward and she fell into the visitor bathroom. Park shut the door. She could hear the door click and Park cursing, less muffled than before.

She stood and shook her head.

"Dammit!" she said, her own voice echoing in her head. It sounded like her ears were full of cotton. "Be careful!"

"You were damned near fucked," said Park, leaning back against the door. "Plus, you made me waste a bullet."

She looked at him and he smirked at her.

She smirked back and rubbed her ear. Her hearing was returning.

"Okay," she said. "We'll need another weapon."

Moaning and scratching came from behind the door.

"Fast, too," said Park, reloading his rifle with the few bullets he had left. He tossed the empty ammo box in the trash. "Or it'll just be a question of deciding if the fire or those fucks outside kill us."

Wisps of smoke came under the door.

"Fire..." said Angie, then looked around. She ran over to the toilet and snatched up the plunger.

Park snorted. "You gonna plunge their brains out with that?"

"Not quite." She twisted the rubber end off the plunger, leaving only the wooden handle. She stepped over to sink and opened the cabinet underneath. She started rooting around in the cabinet.

"I've been thinking," Park said, checking the rifle over.

"Yeah?" said Angie, still looking in the cabinet.

"About why I haven't offed myself yet. You talking about your kids got me to thinking about my girls. They'd be about fourteen by now. When we get out of here, I'm gonna find them. See how they are."

"And how their mother is?"

"Can't say I give a fuck about that. But I guess I'll have to see one to see the other."

Angie found what she was looking for, pulling out a white hospital-issue hand towel. She straightened and wrapped the towel tight around the top of the plunger handle.

"The hell...?" said Park.

Angie took out Park's lighter. She put the plunger handle under her arm and used both hands to snap the plastic casing of the lighter open.

"Hey!" said Park.

"I'll buy you another one," she said. She took the plunger handle from under her arm and poured the lighter fluid over the towel wrapped around its top. "Now, open the door and clear me a path."

Park raised his eyebrows and pushed himself away from the door. "I think I know what you got in mind. You sure about this?"

"Have to be," she said.

"Okay, then."

Park opened the bathroom door and stepped back. A corpse was waiting just behind the door. Park leveled his rifle at the corpse's head and fired. The corpse's head exploded and it fell to the floor. Angie leapt over the falling corpse and ran out into the hallway, heading to the left. Toward the fire.

She felt relief that no corpses were waiting for her. She heard them groan from behind and she heard Park firing, keeping them at bay. How many bullets did he have left?

The smoke stung her nose and eyes as she ran closer to the flames. She hoped no corpses had managed to keep ahead of the fire. She hoped she wouldn't meet a corpse before she found the outer edge of the flames.

To her relief, she met the fire first.

The heat was overwhelming. She saw still corpses, their brains cooked from the heat, lying about ten feet in front of her. Kristen's torn body was among them.

She ignored that as best she could and shoved the plunger handle, towel-end first, into the fire. The towel burst into flame. Angie turned and ran back up the hall, her makeshift torch flashing as she pumped her arms.

Park was aiming for another corpse when she arrived back at the bathroom door.

"Don't waste the bullet!" she yelled, swinging the torch at the nearest corpse. The corpse caught fire. It and the others backed off, back down the hall.

"Well, fuck me!" said Park, lowering the rifle and wiping his forehead. "I half-expected you to burn to death."

"Not yet," she said. "We got kids to get to. Let's move."

* * *

"There it is!" said Maylee, pointing through the trees. The hospital parking lot was lit up just down the hill and across the road. The other side of the hill was free of trees, cleared long ago by road construction. It was a clear run.

Dalton let go of Maylee's hand and started running down the hill. "Come on!"

Maylee gripped her bat and followed.

Her legs pumped under her as she ran through the tall grass of the hill. Dalton was just a few feet ahead. The way was clear. They would be there any minute now and Mom would...

Dalton cried out and fell to the ground.

Maylee didn't have enough time to stop. She tripped over Dalton and sprawled out onto the grass in front of him.

She rolled over and saw Dalton struggling with a fallen corpse in the grass. It was a man in a ruined business suit. Bones protruded from his limp legs. He had one good arm, clutching at Dalton.

Maylee leapt back to her feet and swung golf-style at the man's head. It snapped to one side and he let go of Dalton.

Dalton stood and looked at her. "You're getting scary with that bat."

"Saved your ass," she said, then ran, motioning for him to follow.

Within minutes they were across the street and into the parking lot.

* * *

Angie turned the corner first, holding the torch in front of her. Park stepped out behind her. He had his rifle at the ready, sweeping right and left, looking. Lights flickered. The alarm blared. The smoke was getting thicker around them.

A corpse came for them. Angie slammed her torch into the corpse's head. The corpse caught fire and fell to one side, struggling to get away from both Angie and the flame on its face. A second corpse came for Angie before she could bring the torch around for another blow. Park fired over her shoulder. The corpse's head crumpled inward and it fell.

They walked a few more feet unmolested. A corpse lumbered up to them. A large, muscular man who looked imposing even dead.

Angie blinked at him. "Ed?"

* * *

Maylee hit the parking lot first and kept running, heading for the entrance.

"Hey!" said Dalton, turning to run to the left.

Maylee stopped and cursed. "Dalton! What the fuck? We're here!"

She looked and saw Dalton running to a police car. A door was open. The light bar was still flashing. "A cop, Maylee!" said Dalton, almost to the car. "He can help!"

Maylee sucked in her breath and ran after him. "Dalton, no!"

Dalton reached the police car first. Maylee could see a cop, slumped over in his seat. "Officer?" Dalton said just as Maylee reached him.

The cop looked up and opened his fogged eyes. He hissed at Dalton and reached for him.

Dalton screamed and jumped back. "He's one of them!"

"What a surprise," said Maylee, pushing Dalton back and raising her bat.

The cop leaned forward, still reaching. His torso separated from his legs and fell forward into the parking lot. Blood and ropes of intestines fell out after him.

Maylee and Dalton jumped back in disgust. Maylee whacked him on the head and his jaw slammed into the pavement. She heard a "crack" and the cop was still.

She turned to Dalton, about to speak, then stopped. Moans came from behind where Dalton stood. Dalton heard it and moved to Maylee's side.

"Shit," said Maylee. She leaned into the cop car, doing her best to ignore the bottom half of the cop, and turned on the headlights. They flooded over an approaching group of corpses.

"Oh crap, Maylee, we gotta go," said Dalton, tugging at her hand.

"Not yet. We can't lead these things to Mom." Maylee grabbed the keys in the ignition and started the car.

She straightened back up and pulled her hand free of Dalton.

"What are you doing?" said Dalton.

"This," said Maylee. She grabbed the cop's torso and carried it back to the car. She leaned into the front seat and shoved the torso onto the gas pedal. The engine roared. She pulled the gearshift into drive and jumped back.

The car lurched forward, ramming into the approaching corpses. Groaning and crunching came from in front of and underneath the car.

Maylee turned back to Dalton. "Now we can go."

* * *

Angie stepped back as the corpse of Ed lumbered forward. The smoke around them was getting thicker. The alarm blared. The lights flickered.

"Ed?" said Park. "From the diner?"

Ed groaned and blinked clouded eyes at them. He had a horrible bite wound on his right forearm. The center of the wound was black and thick fluid oozed from it.

"Yeah," said Angie.

Park pointed his rifle at him. "Shall I?"

"I got this one," said Angie. She swung the torch at Ed. Ed groaned and stepped back, swinging his arms at the torch. The torch hit Ed on the wounded arm. The fluid from Ed's wound ran over the flame. The flame sputtered and went out.

"Shit," said Angie.

Ed bit at her, raising a hand to grab.

Park fired. The bullet slammed through Ed's hand and into his skull. Ed let out a long hiss and fell over.

"Shit," Angie repeated, looking ruefully at her ruined torch.

"How much further?" Park asked.

Angie squinted through the gathering smoke. She could make out the edge of the doorway to the emergency room.

"Just up ahead."

* * *

Maylee ran across the parking lot, heading for the door.

She skidded to a halt when she saw the large hole where the ambulance entrance had been.

"Damn," said Dalton, pulling up next to her.

"There," Maylee said. "I bet that's where Mom's headed for. Easiest way out. Come on."

Maylee took a step forward just as a cold hand closed on her arm.

She screamed and spun around to face the corpse. It was a balding man in a doctor's coat. His intestines spilled out of his front, going between his legs and trailing behind him.

"Doctor Gordon?" said Maylee, recognizing him from the few times she had been with Mom at work.

Doctor Gordon groaned and black blood spilled from his mouth. He reached for Maylee.

Maylee screamed and slammed the bat against his head. Dr. Gordon stumbled to the side and fell. Maylee stepped over and slammed his head again. And again. And again. Dr. Gordon was still. Maylee kept slamming down on his head.

Maylee screamed as she brought the bat down. "I am so fucking sick of these fucking things!"

"Maylee..." said Dalton.

Maylee kept slamming down. The bat rang against the pavement. Dr. Gordon's skull was all but completely gone.

"Maylee.."

"What?" Maylee hissed at Dalton, turning to him and panting. Then she looked around. Corpses were coming out of the hole in the side of the hospital. Toward them.

* * *

Angie and Park crept to the entrance to the emergency room. They both cast quick glances around the edge.

Corpses filled the room, wandering around and groaning at nothing. Angie recognized a few patients and a few aides among them. All dead and all hungry.

Angie and Park pulled back.

"Shit," said Park.

"It's still crammed full of those things," said Angie. "How many bullets you got left?"

Park checked, then looked at her. "Fuck."

"What?" said Angie.

"One."

The lights flickered and went out.

"Shit," said Maylee, backing away from the corpses pouring out of the hole. "Let's take the main door after all."

She and Dalton turned to head that way. More corpses came from that direction, hissing and moaning.

"Crap!" said Dalton.

"Here," said Maylee, lifting Dalton up on the hood of the nearest car. "This will buy us some time to think." She climbed up after him.

Dalton clambered to the roof of the car and looked around at the corpses. "Think of what?"

Maylee joined him on the roof and looked around. "I don't know."

The parking lot lights flickered and went out.

*   *   *

Angie and Park crouched in the darkened hallway. The alarm had stopped when the lights went. Angie could hear groaning and could smell smoke. All was dark.

She fished out Freeda's cell phone and flipped it open. The pale blue light from the display lit up Park and the immediate hallway. The display showed her last received call. Brooke's cell phone.

"How long until the back-up generator kicks in?" said Park.

"Not long. Less than a minute. But what the hell do we do when it does?"

Park rubbed his stubble, looked at his rifle, then back at her. "I got an idea."

*   *   *

All around Maylee and Dalton was dark. The moon was gone. Maylee could hear corpses surrounding the car. She could smell them. They groaned and scraped at the metal of the car.

Dalton clung to Maylee. "What are we going to do?"

She blinked away tears. "I don't know."

*   *   *

"Are you insane?" said Angie.

Park shook his head in the pale blue light from the cell phone. "Listen, I do two things. Three if you count jacking off. Cars and guns."

"The ambulance isn't a car, Parker," said Angie.

"Close enough," said Park.

The lights came back, dimmer than before. The fire alarm started blaring again.

"And there's the generator," said Park, grinning and standing. "Come on."

Angie stood. The smoke was thick. The corpses groaned from the emergency room. They were running out of time. "We're both going to die, Park. You know that, right?"

"I know no such thing," said Park. "Make some noise!"

Park ducked around the corner and entered the emergency room.

Angie sighed and ran in after him.

Corpses groaned and turned to Park. Angie started screaming and waving her hands.

"Hey!" she yelled. "Fuckers! Over here!"

Some of the corpses groaned and came for her.

"Hurry!" she yelled and the corpses closed in around her. She was cornered.

* * *

Park looked around the emergency room as he entered. Angie started screaming and waving her arms, drawing some of the corpses away.

He looked at the ambulance. He was facing the front of it. He could see the crushed head of the dispatcher under the front wheel. He was looking for something. Which side would it be on?

He took his best guess and ran for the remains of the dispatch desk. Several corpses reached for him but he knocked them aside. He leapt up onto the smashed desk and looked at the ambulance.

Fuck yeah, he thought. *Gonna see my girls yet.*

He leveled the rifle at the side of the ambulance.

Or more specifically, at the gas tank.

He pulled the trigger.

The force of the ambulance exploding threw Angie against the wall. The corpses surrounding her were knocked forward, falling into her. The fireball flooded their backs and set the corpses alight. The corpses groaned and scattered.

It looked like the whole world was on fire. Thick smoke choked her as she stumbled forward, looking around. Corpses were still groaning and scattering, all of them more concerned with the fire than with her.

"Park?" she yelled.

The fire grew around her. The fire alarm shrieked. Smoke and the smell of burning flesh surrounded her.

"Park?"

Nothing.

* * *

Maylee and Dalton clutched each other in the darkness. Dalton was crying. Maylee was too, but she was fighting to hide it. The corpses were close now. She could hear them groaning and scratching at the car.

She looked up at the sky. It had gone from black to just a hint of dark blue. The sun was coming up.

Great, she thought. *Just in time for us to see the things eat us.*

Then the front of the hospital exploded. Flame shot out into the parking lot, dousing most of the corpses. The corpses groaned and scattered. Away from the fire, each other, and the car.

Maylee let go of Dalton and stood. "What the hell?"

"Who cares?" said Dalton. "Let's go!"

Dalton climbed off the car and ran for the hospital.

Maylee hopped down and followed.

Thirty-Three

Angie looked around one last time for Park, then turned to run outside. She heard movement from behind the smashed remains of the dispatch desk. She stopped and looked. Park's form emerged from behind the desk.

"Park?" she yelled.

Park lumbered forward.

"Shit," said Angie, turning to run.

Park coughed. "Wait for me, dammit!"

Angie sighed and turned back. "Say something quicker next time!"

"Mom!" came a voice from outside.

Maylee.

"Maylee?" yelled Angie. She rushed out of the hole in the wall. The cool morning air hit her. Flaming corpses were scattered around the parking lot. Maylee and Dalton were running toward her.

"Mom!" yelled Dalton.

Angie ran forward after them.

They met and Angie hugged them both as tight as she could. "Are you both alright?"

"Yeah," said Dalton, nodding. "But man do we have a lot of crap to tell you!"

"Me, too," said Angie. Park stepped up behind them, brushing off his hunting jacket and looking around.

Angie looked at Maylee. She looked tired. Dirty, bruised and tired.

"You sure you're okay?" Angie said.

"Yeah," said Maylee, nodding.

"You did good."

Maylee smiled and nodded.

"Damn," said Park, looking around.

Angie looked around too. The lot was scattered with corpses, some of them still moving.

Beyond that, she could see a few corpses stumbling down the road.

Beyond that, corpses wandered the woods near the hospital.

And beyond that, she could see the faintest dots of corpses stumbling on the horizon.

She gripped her kids to her. Tightly. "Well, shit."

www.robertrbest.com
Twitter: @robertrbest

The Whole World Is Dead.

2507351R00099

Printed in Great Britain
by Amazon.co.uk, Ltd.,
Marston Gate.